THE DETERMINED RANGER

There was not much time. From the front of the hotel, a dim battery of lights played into the darkness, and Tipton had that brief distance of light in which to snatch out his Colt and fire—while the bay mare was leaping like a racer for the margin of blackness and safety.

He made that snap shot with speed and precision. Even as he pulled the trigger, he knew that it was a hit—and then he saw the form of Dunleven sag forward upon the neck of the horse.

He himself was instantly in the saddle upon his own mount. The bay drew easily and swiftly away from him, and he was pumping lead vainly after a dancing shadow.

Others rode behind him, but they had started too late, and they were soon discouraged.

But though distanced, Tipton did not surrender. . . .

MAX BRAND®

THE OUTLAW REDEEMER

LEISURE BOOKS   NEW YORK CITY

A LEISURE BOOK ®

March 2004

Published by special arrangement with Golden West Literary Agency.

Dorchester Publishing Co., Inc.
200 Madison Avenue
New York, NY 10016

ISBN 0-8439-5268-7

Printed in the United States of America.

Visit us on the web at www.dorchesterpub.com.

THE OUTLAW
REDEEMER

Table of Contents

The Last Irving

Chapter One

"THE YOUNGER GENERATION"

The rain came down on Irvington like musketry along a battle front. It roared on the distant houses, and it boomed, cannon-like, upon the roof of corrugated iron that covered the warehouse across the street. The rain was a great boon to Irvington and a joy to thirsty farms that, all through the valley, would be drinking it in. The "tanks" where the cattle watered were filling rapidly, now. First their green-slime flats were covered with little puddles which grew to pools, then the surface was sheeted across with brown fluid, rapidly rising. For the wind hung in the southeast and hurried enormous cloud masses up to the slopes of the mountains, where, suddenly chilled, they strove to drop the burden of water in an instant. So Irvington and Irvington Valley benefited.

However, Major John Vincent was ill at ease. He stood in front of the window, glowering, until his breathing had covered it with a thick, white steam. He traced a path through the white spot with his finger, but, instead of looking forth again at the picture of Irvington, Major John Vincent turned away and picked up a telegram that lay upon his desk. Major John Vincent swore. The little yellow slip fluttered to the floor, and the major leaned for it until the handle of his Colt made a lump in the tail of his coat. Then, changing his mind, he kicked it with all his might.

Gently, as though in rebuke of such violence, it rose, turned delicately upon an air current, and came to rest against the windowpane. There was a leak, somewhere. The pane was wet, so that the yellow paper instantly turned dark.

He picked it off; it hung dripping in his hand, but still he could read:

Arriving three twenty-two. May I have an hour of your time?

Archibald Irving

"May you have an hour of my time?" said Major Vincent with frightful irony. "Yes, you may have an hour of my time, but will you pay for that hour? No, you will not!"

He kicked the wet telegram again—this time so successfully that it soared, falling with a squashing sound into the wastebasket.

"Archibald Irving," said the major, lighting an old black pipe. "Irving. . . ."

His mind detached him from his office, from the rain-darkened windows, from the corrugated-iron roof that was smoking across the street—to that time when an Irving struck gold on the headwaters of the creek. No wonder they called the village Irvington, when it could never have existed except for that hardy pioneer. That was two generations ago, which in the United States connotes antiquity. What stung the major was that Archibald Irving was grandson and now sole heir to that name and family. Hence, the kicking of the telegram back and forth.

The square-faced clock in the corner pushed the minute hand closer and closer to the appointed time. At length the major, with a tormented roar, fled from his office and started for the station. He saw the train come into view around the long, easy bend; he saw the double puff of white above the engine, heard the two ear-cracking blasts of the whistle.

The Last Irving

It came shuddering and groaning to a halt beside the platform. A fat woman got off, her arms bulging with parcels that she dropped in the rain to embrace a worn little man. A long, gaunt Negro descended from the smoking car. A plump youth with very blond hair and very pink cheeks jumped down, also, came cheerfully down the platform, swinging his suitcase.

But where was Archibald Irving?

Major John Vincent felt a thrill of unholy joy. Something might have happened farther down the line. He hardly knew what he could hope for—anything that would indefinitely delay the arrival of the said Archie would do.

The engine began to pant, and the wheels started slipping and grinding on the wet, sanded track. No doubt Irving would appear now, suddenly, in the act of huddling himself into his coat, with a pair of suitcases flung after him by friendly hands, followed by the cheerful voices of those who had recently been taking his money at a poker game. Once more in Irvington there would appear a man of that familiar race, tall, big of bone, capable of jaw and hand. . . .

The major began to regret the inhospitable thoughts that had recently been making rebellion in his soul. Like all true men of Irvington, there was in him a spark of loyalty to the blood of the founder. But here was the train puffing, staggering, and now lurching ahead with gathering speed.

He began to watch with an eager expectancy. It surely seemed, in his eye, that the train was already traveling at such a rate that it insured a broken leg or a fractured ankle to anyone who dared to attempt to drop to the ground. But then the Irvings were a race who never failed to do the unexpected and the startling. The major began to stand upon one foot, like a man watching his horse come down the homestretch following just a little to the rear of the leader.

Now the train had gathered such momentum that it was flying along at the rate of forty or forty-five miles an hour, and still not a sign of a descending passenger.

Obviously, thought the major, young Irving was very drunk, and had ridden past his station. The major grinned. He himself had been young, and even now his spirit was not so very old. He decided that, if the boy were really of the right stuff, he would go to no limit of trouble to set him on his feet in the valley and start him again toward a comfortable estate in life. However, the third generation from the pioneering stuff was apt to be. . . .

With an oath, the major turned; a foolish, careless whistling had been dinning into his ears all this while. The whistler was the blond, plump youth whom Vincent had noted before with a cigarette hanging from his fingers, his eyes filled with the blankness of the music-maker, while he blew with shrill power:

> **Shuffle up them coffin lids;**
> **Bring me to them ragtime kids. . . .**

Major Vincent did not like ragtime. He was of the generation that preferred its sentimentality in a more languid form, a little sickly. . . . The major told himself that this smart young fellow typified the lighter, vainer, more useless generation that had come to supplant their elders.

"You're John Vincent," said the youth.

A frightful thought stabbed the major to the heart. He could not speak.

The plump youth added: "I'm Archibald Irving."

The major raised a hand heavier than lead and clasped that of the stranger. Then he led him dolefully from the station platform.

"Hello, Major. . . ."

This came from somewhere, and the major waved a blind hand.

"You were in the war, then," young Archibald was saying. "And you came out a major?"

"My grandfather was a general in some sort of a war," explained Vincent, "which made my father a colonel when he was thirty, and so, when I was thirty, I naturally inherited the title of major."

Archibald grinned.

"But where," he asked, "are the pawing bronchos standing at the hitching posts? Where are the languid cowpunchers leaking local color and tobacco . . . where are the gilded spurs and the six-guns and . . . ?"

"The devil!" said the lawyer.

"Oh," said Archibald, "is it as bad as that? Nothing but flivvers, now?"

The major could not decide whether or not he would smile upon such flippancy. When he had churned the handle of his own car and stepped into the front seat beside his passenger, he relaxed enough to say: "You shake a real car to pieces trying to jump from hill to hill with it, the way you have to do out here. But you take a flivver . . . it's just as much at home among the rocks as on the level. . . ."

"I like a flivver," said Archibald, "because they keep you company. What does one of those big, heavy cars do but hiss at you when you pet it and try to jump out from under you? A fliv always talks right back to you. And you generally know where to find them. They may buck, but they won't run very far."

The lawyer turned a little in the seat and scanned his companion again.

"Which college was it?" he said.

"Nothing of any importance," said Archibald.

"Humph!" exclaimed the lawyer. "I hope that you didn't waste your money when you went to college."

"Oh, not at all, not at all," said Archibald. "I learned a lot in the old dive."

"In the which?" asked the lawyer. "But go right ahead. Don't let me interrupt. What did you learn?"

"To make myself at home," said Archibald, "and to take advantage of opportunities. Have you got the makings to spare?"

The major grinned again and passed over tobacco sack and papers.

"Where did you learn that art," he queried, as he watched Archibald's fat fingers construct a cigarette with flawless speed. "Where did you learn that . . . on your uncle's allowance?"

"My allowance," said Archibald, "never got me past the fifth of the month."

"Good heavens!" cried the major. "Not on three hundred per?"

"You know how it is," confided Archibald. "You run a bit behind and borrow a trifle, and then the next month you pay it all back . . . which makes your credit good . . . you understand?"

The lawyer swallowed. He said: "When I was in college, my allowance was thirty dollars a month. And I had my fun, too."

"Well," remarked Archibald, "you must have been a credit to your family."

The major looked askance. Archibald's eye was as guileless, as blue, and as empty as the eye of a china duck. The major concluded in his heart of hearts: *This lad is a fool and doesn't care who knows it.*

Chapter Two

"FAMILY HISTORY"

The rain had not stopped falling. By the time they got into Mr. Vincent's office enough had fallen to sprinkle Archibald's gray flannel coat. But in this young man there burned a fire of good cheer with so steady a flame that it could not easily be dimmed.

"Now," said Mr. Vincent kindly, "you know that I have always been your uncle's lawyer, and that my father was the lawyer of your granduncle. So I think I can tell you to open up and fire away. Tell me about yourself."

"Why," said Archibald, "there isn't much to tell, you know."

And the lawyer believed that Archibald had scored a bull's-eye.

"At least," Vincent continued, "I can guess why you've come here. You were disappointed by the small size of the inheritance. You naturally want to look affairs over and make up your mind for yourself."

"That's why I started," said young Mr. Irving. "But on the way I changed my mind. I like this country pretty well. I may decide to live out here."

"May I ask what you know about this country?"

"I've traveled through about a thousand miles of it on the train," said Archibald. "That's something, I suppose."

The former opinion of Vincent was reinforced.

"And you like the look of it?" asked the lawyer.

"Oh, yes. Jolly old bald-faced hills. Lots of room. There's

only one real trouble."

"You surprise and delight me," said Major Vincent. "What is the only failing, may I ask?"

"There are hardly enough fences for jumping," said Archibald. "At least, not in the districts that I have seen so far."

The lawyer rose and strode to the window. Then he strode back again and sat down. "There are plenty of foxes, though," he said.

"Why," said Archibald with enthusiasm, "that's good news, really. If there are foxes, there must be a way to have fun catching them."

"Unless they catch you first," said the lawyer.

"I don't understand," said Archibald.

"Experience is the only teacher for some," said Vincent. "So you are going to settle down out here?"

"I am thinking of it."

"There isn't much of a house."

"Oh," said Archibald. "That's just the point, you see . . . I want to find a simple place. Altogether, I've got about twenty-four hundred a year . . . and back East that's nothing. Out here it ought to keep a house and a dog or two. What?"

Mr. Vincent sighed. "You had better look things over for yourself," he said. "Suppose you let me drive you out to your place?"

The flivver placed them swiftly in the open country. There were not enough trees to be worth speaking of. Spanish daggers were the greatest plants, and they bristled in hill and dale like wretched stakes. The drenching rain had taken from the landscape its usual burned and baked appearance, but it had turned the mud black as a mourning garment.

"Here," said the lawyer, "your grandfather's land began.

Your father had that share yonder. . . ."

The car had stopped at the mouth of a vast amphitheater, a dozen miles from lip to lip. Two little streams ran down the opposite slopes, fringed thinly with trees, and joined in a small lake in the center of the hollow.

"Your father had that share yonder, where you see the lake . . . all to the north of that, with the stream running through it. Your Uncle Edward had this southern half. Your father sold his bit to the Pierces, the Dunvegans, and the rest of them . . . you can see their houses, yonder, where the shadows of the trees are. However, this is all old, stale history to you."

"Not at all," said Archibald. "I never heard it before . . . that I remember. Never had any head for history, you see. What a fine swing for the hounds it would be, across this valley."

"It would," said the lawyer, and set his jaw. He continued: "That left your Uncle Edward as the only representative of the family in Irving Valley. He had this great chunk . . . let me see . . . I suppose close to forty thousand acres, in all. Good acres, too. Very good acres. Why, you can see for yourself, where old Fraser has broken ground down there on the shores of the lake. You can see the blackness, even from this distance. He's just plowed it. That land had its value for cattle. Very good value. But under the plow it will be worth more than a hundred an acre. I don't mean that the whole valley is worth that. We don't know, yet. But old Fraser . . . the fox . . . has started cultivating fifteen hundred acres there by the lake. And they'll pay . . . oh, they'll pay big. I should say that his first crop will give him a profit of twenty dollars an acre. Yes, I should say that the fifteen hundred acres there by the lake . . . just that bit alone . . . must be worth nigh onto two-hundred-thousand dollars. . . ."

"Twelve thousand a year," said Archibald, translating

thoughtfully into the terms that interested him most. "Or ten thousand, putting the capital into sure things, only. Still, a man could do on ten thousand . . . by cutting the corners, a little."

The lawyer gave a cutting side glance to his young companion.

"I should think that a man could do on that," he agreed. "Well, *you* may even have to learn to do on less."

"Oh, yes, for a while," said Archibald. "Until I turn my hand to something."

"You're going to be a money-maker?" queried Vincent with deep sarcasm. "You're going to pick up a little fortune for yourself, after a time, are you?"

"Have to have money to live happily, you know," said Archibald. "And there must be ways of doing it. There must be ways. A big country, and a pretty new one. After all, it was only fifty years ago that my grandfather came out here and found it all unclaimed."

"He was partly a lucky man and partly a great man," said Vincent. "I hope that some of his blood really runs in you."

"But it does, you know . . . I don't mean the greatness, but I've always had luck."

"At what?" snapped out Vincent.

"At bridge," said luckless Archibald. And he began to whistle again:

> **Shuffle up them coffin lids;**
> **Bring along them ragtime kids. . . .**

"I suppose you're tired of all this dull talk," said Vincent.

"Oh, no. I'm frightfully interested. What did Dad sell for?"

"Three hundred and fifty thousand . . . and because his wife wanted to go back East. By the way, do you resemble your mother at all?"

"Ringer for her," said Archibald cheerfully.

"I thought so," said his uncle's lawyer. "Very well. He sold, and that money he dropped somewhere in the East. . . ."

"Somewhere between Forty-Second and Broadway and Florida. He planted it pretty carefully," said Archibald. "He sowed it so deep, though, that it never grew a crop for him. But he had a fine time in the planting season. Good old Dad!" And he chuckled in a mellowed appreciation of these admirable qualities in his father.

"And then," snapped out the lawyer, "your uncle came to your rescue, just as you were left stranded, and gave you two hundred a month for spending money in your preparatory school. . . ."

"I only owed five hundred when I graduated," said Archibald.

With this oblique answer, Mr. Vincent was forced to content himself.

"To go on with your Uncle Edward. He was rather a careless businessman but not a bad one. I mean, he had good ideas. But he didn't turn those ideas into money quite fast enough. He kept taking money out of the place and putting in machinery . . . tractors, plows. He was always building a road, or putting up a better style of fence, or selling off one brand of cows and putting a fine run of high bloods in their place . . . or building a new addition onto the barns, or constructing new corrals. Finally he got the farming bug in his head, and that was really the finish of him."

"Ah," said young Archibald, pointing, "that black strip by the lake *does* look like a mourning badge, doesn't it? But how did the farming ruin him?"

"He started at the wrong end of farming, you know. He began by putting in machinery . . . tractors, plows, and such stuff. He cut big irrigation and drainage ditches, and he bought huge circular pumps that were to suck the water up from the lake and bring it onto the higher lands, even up as far as this, you understand? What your uncle was seeing was not simply that patch of black land down there by the lake under cultivation. For he had a vision of this whole valley turned into a green bowl . . . oranges, lemons, almonds, and fine cherries. There was no end to his dream for this valley, because he said that the slope was not so great as to prevent the checking of the entire valley for irrigation, there was good depth of fine soil everywhere, and there was a hot sun to pull up trees and alfalfa fast. Nothing needed except, of course, water, and yonder was the water and had been . . . for some hundreds of thousands of years."

"I begin to see," said Archibald.

"Good for you," said the lawyer bitterly. "Your uncle bought so much and got so ready for this work of his that he even went so far as to secure options on all of the lands that had once belonged to your grandfather . . . options on the whole valley, and those options have not yet run out . . . and they *won't* run out for another five years . . . because the old fellow gambled deep. When he had the materials all spread out and was about to actually put the paint upon the canvas, he found that the paint was not ready . . . and that he had to have it. In one word, he was overextended. . . ."

"It seems to me that I have seen that word before," said Archibald innocently.

"In your third reader, perhaps," said the bitter lawyer. "However, you had better learn about these things, if you expect to reconstruct the family fortunes."

"Of course," said Archibald, "I must do that. I owe it to my father and my kind uncle, you might say."

The lawyer gasped. But Archibald was merely yawning.

Chapter Three

" 'SHUFFLE UP THEM COFFIN LIDS' "

"And when my Uncle Edward overextended himself . . . he lost his balance, so to speak?"

John Vincent replied in a voice that was a growl: "Young man, he went practically broke!"

"Hard luck," said the youth.

"Robbery," said his elder.

"Robbery?" said Archie.

"Robbery!" roared the lawyer, and he jammed in the gear-shift lever, sending the flivver away with a lurch and a roar.

"You mean . . . that a gun was put to his head?" asked Archie.

"I mean . . . that he owed a miserable fifty thousand dollars to two men. He had tools on the place . . . engines and machines of various sorts, tractors and plows and harrows and what not . . . that had a value of close to a hundred thousand dollars. The paint on them was not even scratched. He had land alone which was worth more than half a million. On top of all that, he had a good house, fine buildings and barns around it, and a gorgeous lot of cattle of the very first quality. Considering what *could* be done with his half of the valley, in the way of improvements, I say that your uncle at that moment was worth at least a cold million minus the wretched little fifty thousand that he had borrowed from those two buzzards!"

He raised his fist and jammed it down on the steering

wheel with such force that the entire front end of the car shivered. In his day, the lawyer had been a farmhand, and he still had a mighty forearm to show for it. Pudgy little Mr. Irving gasped, round-eyed, at this display of passion and of power.

"Well," he said, "it begins to sound like a book. I think that probably my uncle did not have quite fair play."

"You think!" exclaimed terrible John Vincent. "You think that maybe he did not have fair play? Well, young man, the value of the options on that land across the valley could be variously estimated, too. That land, as it stands, lake lands and bottomland by the river, and all, ought to be worth about a hundred and eighty thousand dollars. But improved . . . I want the world to hear me stand up and shout that that same land is worth eight-hundred-thousand dollars . . . which might be stretched to *another* million.

"Now, then, my friend, I want you to contemplate the picture for yourself. Here is a man with the prospect of a million right under his nose, and the prospect of a profit of from six to eight-hundred-thousand dollars in addition from the lands on the other half of the valley. Beyond that, he has before him the chance of realizing a tidy dream. Not Napoléonic, maybe, but with a hope of doing the world a lot more concrete good than any Napoléon ever did . . . a hope, you see, of making these twelve-thousand acres become a regular garden. And himself and his house in the middle of the garden, like a king with a great house . . . right on the edge of that lake . . . and he intended to have his little sailing boat and his launch on that lake. With a little clearing out of the bottom, the river could be made navigable clear down to the town . . . why, it would have been like living as a prince in a principality that one has built up for oneself!"

"Humph!" said young Irving.

"It doesn't seem to appeal to you greatly," said the lawyer.

"Did you say that he intended to put most of the land in fruit?"

"You don't like fruit, perhaps?"

"Twelve-thousand acres of plowed ground . . . it would raise the very devil with any hunting, you know. A fox would just head for this valley . . . and the horses would be blown inside of five minutes. . . ."

He shook his head, while the lawyer looked around with a faint smile, as though ready to be slightly amused by this remark if it were a jest. But the eye of young Irving remained as clear and as blank a blue as ever. The lawyer jerked his head back again and began to curse frightfully through his gripped teeth.

"A bad road, isn't it?" said Archibald with much sympathy.

"A devil of a road," said the lawyer.

"However," said Archibald, "he *didn't* plant the trees, after all."

"No," said the lawyer, "he was smashed just as he had the door open, and just as he was about to step forward to a great success . . . poor Ned. He was a fine fellow . . . a grand man. God bless him!"

"However," said young Archibald, "since he had only such a very short time to live and enjoy his work . . . it hardly mattered that he wasn't able to push it through a little earlier. . . ."

"Young Mister Irving, very young Mister Irving," said the other, "may I try to make you understand that this death of your uncle was due to a broken heart?"

"A broken heart?" asked Mr. Irving. "Dash me! A broken heart? How romantic! And in my own family? No one would hardly believe such a thing. Really?"

"No doubt," said Mr. Vincent, "they would not. However, I am telling you the facts of the matter."

"Thank you a thousand times," said Archibald. "It is a lot better than a book . . . better than most books, anyway. Please go on."

The lawyer loosened his collar. Finally he said: "Yes, I'll get it over, done with, and off my hands. I say that your uncle ran short of cash because he was simply about a year too premature in laying in his supply of tools for improving the valley lands. He had to have more cash, and he went to the two richest men in the county . . . or in any of the five counties around you. He got twenty-five-thousand dollars from Fraser, the banker, and he got twenty-five-thousand dollars from Bill Watson, the rancher."

"If they were both so rich," said young Irving, "I should think that poor Uncle Ned could have saved a frightful lot of time and trouble by borrowing it all from one of them and letting the other alone."

"You would think that, if you didn't know the situation. But that pair are the only two aces in this pack. They own everything on each side of Irving Valley. They hate each other like the worst poisons. They're crooks, both of them. And each one is smart enough to do everybody except the other one. Watson knows a lot more about land and cattle . . . but Fraser has it all over Watson when it comes to such matters as straight finance . . . the getting in and the letting out of money. So that now Fraser has just as much land as Watson . . . or very nearly as much . . . and in addition to that he has his bank, which is a pretty tidy item all by itself. In a word, young man, Fraser has his hands on Irvington and about half of the country around it. Watson has the other half. Oh, there are other people, of course, and lots of them, but this pair has the choice bits, and they're picking up the rest, between them, pretty rapidly. White men are leaving

Irvington and the country around it. And here's one white man that's going to go on the outward trail before long. I'm licked. The rest of them are licked. All licked! And by those two spavined, roach-backed, broken-down old scoundrels! Bah! I despise myself when I think about it!"

"I'm frightfully sorry," said Archibald, and lighted another cigarette.

"So your uncle didn't want to offend one of these ogres by doing all of his borrowing from the other. Both were money lenders, and both of them liked to be patronized. He got twenty-five thousand from each of them. And that was that."

"It seems quite complicated. So many names," said Archibald.

The lawyer swallowed his fury and went on: "He had that money on a short-term loan . . . which was a piece of folly in the first place. And I told him so. Oh, I told him so. But he was determined. He wanted to get the money, and he was always certain that the valley would turn a miracle for him. The money came nearly due, and the miracle was not happening. So your uncle got ready to raise money from another quarter to meet those two short loans.

"He had his grip packed for a trip to the East, and he was about to start, when it popped into his mind that he might as well try the two old devils before he spent so much time on such a trip . . . when his time was doubly valuable in the valley, superintending operations. Hey . . . there goes old Fraser now!"

A long-bodied, dark-blue automobile whirred down the road past them, and young Irving had a glimpse of a white head in the driver's seat.

"That's his one dissipation. He loves an automobile that can jump along the road. Well, as I was saying, your Uncle Ned first went to find Watson, because Watson is supposed to be a little the more human of the pair. But Watson wasn't home, and so he went to Fraser, and told Fraser simply that he knew the note was coming due, and that he wanted to know if Fraser would extend it when the time came. Fraser, the villain, said that he would, and your poor childish uncle trusted to the word of that crocodile and did not get the promise reduced to writing. You see the whole conclusion, now."

"No, I don't."

"Really? Well, Archibald Irving, when the note came due, your uncle went to Fraser and said he had come to get the note extended . . . and the infernal old hypocrite, of course, wrung his hands and swore that his heart was broken with grief, but that a number of bad deals had gone through . . . and that he could not extend the note."

The lawyer paused, breathing hard, and then he went on: "Of course, your Uncle Ned was not simpleton enough to have any doubts. He knew that he was about to be done, and he did not argue. He walked out of the office of the shark and came to mine. I thought the thing over and saw that it was a pretty nasty pickle. Because, you see, fifty thousand dollars is a fairly sizable loan, and it would take a long time to make an Eastern bank take kindly to such an idea. American banking is really pretty conservative. The English are your great bankers. They will gamble on long chances, but the American bank is very crusty. It can afford to be, because for a century it has had the finest securities that the world ever saw in its hands.

"I saw that there was no chance to raise a quick fifty thousand dollar loan in local quarters, because the only big money around Irvington was that which was in the hands of Fraser . . . except for the money which Watson had already tied up.

"Just there I thought that I had an inspiration. It seemed to me that Watson would nearly die of rage and of envy, if he knew that the banker was about to foreclose on the valley for a wretched twenty-five thousand dollar mortgage. So we started over to see Watson, hoping to make him a generous Watson, not because of a great heart, but because it would poison him to think that his rival should get any advantage over him.

"And here came another blow . . . for we found that Watson had gone out, having been called away on business . . . leaving word to close down for the twenty-five thousand that was owed by your uncle on the dot.

"It was bitter, hard luck. If we could have got to Watson, I know perfectly well that he would certainly have been glad to stall off Mister Fraser by extending money to cover both loans. But he was out of hand, and, before that day closed, your uncle's notes were overdue. After that . . . well, there's no use going into the dirty details. Watson was away. . . . Ah, there he goes."

Another long blue-bodied car lounged up the road.

"Watson changes his style of automobile whenever old Fraser does. Not that he likes cars, but because he won't have Fraser put anything over on him . . . even in style of cars. He duplicates Fraser's buy every time. Well, bad luck to them both! But there was your Uncle Ned, caught to rights. And the long and short of it was that he had to sell to meet those debts . . . oh, yes, they made him sell. They made him sell his tools, which were so new and good . . . though, of course, they only brought ten per cent at second-hand. They made him sell his cattle, though it was the off season . . . in a word, my son, the only people who were able to bid on a property of that size were old Fraser and old Watson, and the Watson devil was still out of the country! The result was that Fraser had nothing to bid against except his shame, and shame was never a very eloquent matter with him.

"What he did was to offer the fifty thousand for the notes, and forty thousand in cash besides, together with the home and the buildings standing around it.

"Yes, sir, though no one could possibly believe in such a thing, I give you my word that all that infernal old skinflint would offer for an estate worth half a million in cold cash as it stood . . . and worth a large million in prospect . . . was a wretched ninety-thousand dollars . . . of which he had to put out only sixty-five thousand in cash.

"It breaks a man's heart to think of it. Aye, and it broke your uncle's heart, and no wonder. He didn't live for a month after that sale. And he was like a stunned man from the day that the notes came due and were not paid."

"Dear me," said Archibald, "if he had only had a few friends. . . ."

"Friends? My boy, every man in the county was his friend."

"And there isn't fifty thousand dollars in the county?" said young Irving.

The lawyer caught his breath, started to answer, and then looked swiftly aside at his companion, as though for the first time he began to doubt his former opinion of the heir of the famous name of Irving. However, that doubt vanished like a cloud shadow and was gone. For young Mr. Irving pursed his lips and swelled his cheeks and began to whistle merrily:

Shuffle up them coffin lids. . . .

Chapter Four

"TWO OLD SQUIRRELS"

They went down to the edge of the lake and into the house that stood gloomily there at the edge of the water. They climbed up to the porch and looked through the windows, and then the lawyer unlocked the front door, and they wandered through room after room.

"Like a stable, you know," said Archibald.

"Yes," replied the lawyer, "because your uncle was a working man."

"Oh, well," said Archibald, "one needn't be so very gloomy about one's work, do you think?"

"Bah!" exclaimed the lawyer.

"I didn't quite hear you," said Archibald.

"I'm getting a cold," said John Vincent, and led the way up the stairs.

He showed the rooms in procession, one by one—big, airy rooms, with lofty ceilings and with French doors that reached from floor to ceiling in turn, filling every nook and cranny of the house with oceans of flooding light. Very little was needed to turn that place into a delightful home except the final luxurious touches of rugs and paintings and comfortable chairs.

"Ned wanted to wait until the valley was opened up," said the lawyer. "Then he would have furnished the house out of the income that the valley itself produced."

"Very neat, sentimental idea," said young Irving. "What's this?"

"The door to the look-out tower. That was one of his ideas. You see, the house climbs up from the lake along the side of a hillock and to the top of it. This tower rises four tall stories, or about sixty feet, from the top of the hill, so that, when you stand on the top platform, you can sweep the whole country rather thoroughly. Your uncle liked that. He was in the habit of walking up and down on the platform at the close of every day, thinking over what work had been done and what work was still to do. He could see nearly every inch of the valley from that place, and he could make his plans while he walked there, or while he sat and smoked. . . ."

"Let's have a look at his thoughts, then," interrupted Archibald.

They slowly climbed up the winding staircase toward the roof. It was a plain platform with a plain wooden railing around.

"A stone parapet, someday," Vincent explained.

"And a telescope," said Archibald, "to look around and see what each of the laborers was doing?"

"Yes," said Vincent, "a telescope, but not for that. He had a bit of a leaning toward astronomy. He liked to stare at the stars. And so he spent a good deal of money in having this high-powered glass. . . . Hey, let's get back to shelter!"

The rain turned the air suddenly black with the steady violence of its downpouring. But that rattling shower lasted only a moment. Then the changing wind cuffed the clouds apart, and the sky began to clear rapidly. For a long rain would have been an anomaly at Irvington or in Irving Valley.

Young Archibald Irving, as the air grew clearer, marked with his eye all the features of the valley that stretched around him in almost a perfect circle with a six-mile radius. He could see every building raised on the easy slope of the valley walls. He could see every shrub, well-nigh. Altogether, one might have thought that even the heart of the fox hunter, in plump Mr. Irving, would have quickened a few beats to the minute as he stared at this wide prospect that might one day have come to him, enriched with circling rows of fruit trees, watered from the lake, and made into a garden incredibly rich by the wisdom and the vision and the practical hard labor of his uncle.

But as he walked up and down the platform, Archibald Irving was still whistling lightly until, far away on the side of the southern hill, he saw two little streaks of dark blue. He paused for a moment and gazed at them meditatively.

"There you are!" said the lawyer, with a chuckle, as he followed the direction of Archibald's gaze. "Someday those old codgers will brain one another, they're so filled with hatred and with jealousy. Someday that's what will happen! I wish it would happen tomorrow. Because that day will set free a lot of poor, sweating devils who are in fire for them now. They're snarling at each other up there on the hillside . . . you see, that's the dividing boundary between the two estates . . . the Watson estate and the Fraser estate."

"I don't see," said Archibald, "exactly how Watson got his share of the loot if Fraser did the buying. . . ."

"Don't you? Neither do a lot of others, but the fact is that Watson paid about four hundred and twenty-five thousand dollars for that half of this side of the valley. And if he would pay that price, you can make a guess that it was worth every penny of that sum. You can guess, also, about how much value would have been put on the entire valley, according to your uncle's options. But Watson could not stand the idea that Fraser had slipped in and picked such a perfect plum. Even if he paid its full value, Watson had to have his half, and he got it. But that made one more excellent reason for the pair of them to hate one another. And if they don't get their brains blown out by some maddened debtor, one of these days, they'll die of mutual poison, there's no doubt of that."

"Every man," said young Irving, "has to have his own line of sport . . . and theirs seems to be hating. If this platform were a little larger, one could give a very snug rag party up here under the stars, Vincent. What?"

"What?"

"Don't you dance?"

"No, no! Confound it. . . ."

"Well?"

"Nothing. Nothing! But this house belongs to you, Irving, and, if you want to, you can afford to give a rag party up here, now and then . . . and while you dance, you can look around at the little kingdom that might have been yours. That will make you a lot jollier."

"Exactly," said Archibald, delighted with this sympathy. "And then, I could put the orchestra down there on the lawn. . . ."

"Where will you get the orchestra?" said Vincent. "However, that's your business. Not mine. I'm going back to town. Are you ready to come along?"

"I'm ready to come along, of course. Only . . . well, I'll be with you in a moment."

When John Vincent reached his flivver, he had time to climb into it, climb out again, start the engine, and let the machine idle. He had time to experiment with the degree of slowness to which he could cut down its running as it stood there; he had time to carry on this experiment until the engine actually stopped and had to be cranked and sent off again with a startling roar.

Finally he stood up on the running board, and what did he see? The long muzzle of the big telescope was pointing over the side of the high platform and was fixed upon the distant hillside.

The Last Irving

"Irving, are you coming?" yelled the justly irritated lawyer.

"Oh . . . terribly sorry . . . coming right away."

There was no dismay and no hurry in the voice. And when young Mr. Irving appeared at the front door again, he was not panting with his haste.

Vincent was gloomy, indeed, as he sent the car back toward Irvington. "You found that telescope amusing, I suppose," he said dryly, "and you didn't realize how time was flying."

"Exactly," said Irving through a yawn. "You see, you can find out things with a telescope."

"Really? That's news," remarked the lawyer. "What sort of things, may I ask?"

"Oh, I looked at a pine tree," said the youth.

"*Humph!* And you saw the tree had a cone in it?"

"No, a squirrel . . . a pair of squirrels! I saw them very clearly . . . a pair of old squirrels." And he laughed. "A funny sight," he said, "to see them playing together."

He seemed so highly contented with his ride into the country, in fact, that he was still gay and smiling as he stepped from the car to the curb in front of the Irvington Hotel. He was whistling as he waved farewell and thanks to John Vincent. As he signed his name on the hotel register, he still smiled, and, when he was shown to his room, he entered it chuckling softly.

It was a very old pair of squirrels that he had seen on the hillside. Each of them, in fact, had a white head.

They were walking back and forth between two great, long-bodied blue automobiles—just the pair of them alone. The most interesting detail of all was that their arms were linking jovially together, in sign of mutual happiness, mutual content.

Chapter Five

"SPIRIT OF THE WEST"

Now that the rain was definitely ended, the sun began to shine, doing a thoroughly Western job of it. In half an hour, all the roofs of Irvington were steaming, although there was only the slant light from the west to heat them.

From the little square on which the hotel and the other chief buildings of Irvington face, there went up a soft, crinkling sound as the sands drank the rainwater deeper and deeper. People began to come tentatively out from the houses and sit on porches. Down the streets into the plaza a horseman came at a pounding gallop, from time to time, perhaps with his poncho still furled over his shoulders.

People began to say: "This rain'll do a lot of good."

Seated at the window in his room, tapping his plump fingertips against the broad arm of his chair, Archibald Irving enjoyed the beauty of the mist rising from the roofs and the brown swelling of the hills, beyond which Irving Valley lay—and the wrecked hopes of his dead uncle. No one could ever have guessed at sorrow so far as Archie was concerned. There was no shadow in his eye; there was no wrinkle in his fat brow. The eternal smile was on his lips, the smile of the thoughtless man.

"So this is the West," said Archie.

He got up and went to the window. The hardware store's delivery wagon went rattling and crashing by, with a freckled boy on the driver's seat. And yonder, a great five-ton truck, with bags of cement heaped heavily on it, was snorting and heaving its way across the plaza, leaving enormous indentations in the rain-softened sand.

"This is the West!" exclaimed Archie, and chuckled.

A pair of newsboys raced out to either end of the block, a pack of their wares under their arms, and they began to make skillful dissonance: "Big train wreck . . . forty-two killed. Read about it now. Get it red hot. Aw . . . *train* wreck. Forty-two killed!"

Tossing their voices back and forth as skillfully as any metropolitan newsies who, in the cañoned streets of Manhattan, make it seem that two or three shouting newspaper vendors are a whole army of prophets with a message of universal woe, so these two worked the little town of Irvington.

Archie sauntered down the stairs, and entered the lobby. In the Western hotel lobbies of which one read in fiction, bespurred men lolled about in crippled chairs, chewing tobacco, rolling cigarettes; there were many guns; there were quiet voices with a snarling menace in them.

Where were these interesting items in the Irvington Hotel?

Alas, they were gone! Yonder, two drummers sat in busy conversation—"I says to the blonde . . . 'Hello, cutie, are you lost?' And she says . . . 'Hello, big boy! You look sort of away from home yourself.' "

No, this was not Western talk; it might have been transplanted from Chicago the very day before. Archie Irving went out to the verandah. A withered little man with a drawn, tired face had a chair tilted back against the wall of the building. There were overalls and a flannel shirt and a ragged-looking silk bandanna to make up his outfit, together with a green, faded hat of black felt, *not* wide of brim, and a pair of rusty spurs on his heels. He held between the fingers of his left hand a wisp of a cigarette. This, then, was a cowpuncher.

Yes, for the inside of the legs of his overalls were polished and polished again by constant rubbing against the stirrup leathers. Alas for romance!

"It won't live," said Archie to himself, "except where a fox pack is hunting . . . it certainly won't live in this century."

The little man stood up and went to lean against a pillar of the hotel verandah and roll another cigarette. His pale, disinterested eyes squinted wearily across the plaza while his trained fingers constructed the smoke without thought and without haste.

How much of his life must be mere matter of habit, thought Archie Irving. Where was the bulge of the gun, supposed to be vaguely outlined near the hip pocket—usually on the right side? No, there was no sign of a gun about him. He was just a tired, gloomy little laborer, whose habitual labor happened to be the chasing of cows across the ranges.

A buckboard was rattling into the plaza and turning toward the hotel. Not the buckboard of the days of romance, with a pair of foam-freckled, little, devilish mustangs furnishing the motive power—but a 20th Century buckboard with an engine tugging the wheels along more faithfully, more swiftly, more strongly, more noisily, than any span of mustangs that ever breathed the prairie air.

The little truck came to a halt with a screech of brakes, a jingle of wire, a rattle of tin—and the lumbering driver leaped down, took a heavy sack of something from the truck body, and shouldered it around toward the rear entrance of the hotel.

"You're an old-timer around here, I s'pose," said Archie to the little cowpuncher.

"Yes, sir, I'm quite an old hand," said the little man. "Might you be a stranger?"

"I haven't seen much of Irvington," said Archie, "except

the station, the hotel, and Watson and Fraser."

"If you seen them two," said the tired voice of the little man, "I guess that you've seen about nine-tenths of this here country. I guess you must have seen them going in opposite directions, eh?"

"That's right. I understand they're not very friendly."

"It's the one reason that the rest of us keep hanging on here . . . because we got a hope that maybe one of those old boys will get enough meanness in his system to finish off the other one. They sure hate each other."

The picture of the two old men, circularly framed in the telescope, walking back and forth arm in arm, came to Archie's mind. He merely said: "I suppose that they've done each other a lot of harm, then?"

"Oh, yes! Never a month goes by that they don't get in a dig at each other."

"Like what?" asked Archie.

"Why, last month there was bidding on the work of building the schoolhouse. When Fraser's building contractor turned in his bid, Watson's contractor cut down under him pretty near ten percent. Just for meanness, for the sake of not having Fraser's man get the job. Even if Watson has got to lose money in the job."

"They even do building contracting, then?"

"Stranger, they even do everything. Watson bought one newspaper so's he could call Fraser names, and then Fraser, he bought up the other newspaper so's he could call Watson names. Every time Fraser backs one man for Congress or school superintendent, or something, Watson backs the other fellow, no matter how bad he may be.

"Fraser owns the big garage, and Watson owns the big repair shop. Fraser has the lumberyard, and Watson has the brick oven. Watson owns the candy store, and Fraser owns the ice cream parlor. Fraser owns the bakery, and Watson owns the flour mill. And that's the way it goes all the way down the line."

"But it seems to me," said Archibald Irving, "that they really own things that don't compete."

"Don't you never doubt none that they don't compete," said the little cowpuncher, with a wise shake of his head. "Fact is, if it wasn't knowed by other folks how terrible hard Watson and Fraser is competing over here, *other* folks might want to come in here and try to make a little competition . . . this being a growing town, like it is. Y'understand?"

Archibald nodded. Still he persisted in seeing the picture of the two old men, arm locked in friendly arm. He could not help remembering that a garage does not necessarily have to compete with a repair shop, and a bakery does not really have to exist by cutting the throat of a flour mill.

"I disremember," said the little cowpuncher, "how long ago it was that I first got a job for Watson, but when. . . . Excuse me just a minute, stranger, will you?"

The little man sauntered to the edge of the porch just as the driver of the "buckboard" came striding around from behind the hotel.

"Hello, Jerry," he said genially.

The big man wheeled and crouched, and a hand darted back toward a hip pocket. But when he saw that the little fellow was standing there with his hands hanging harmlessly at his side, big Jerry straightened, a notch at a time.

"Well, you're here, are you?" said Jerry heavily. "You're here, Doc, are you?"

"I thought that I would just slide in town here and rest up for a time before. . . ."

"Before what?"

"Before I went back to ask you some questions that maybe

you would be sort of curious to hear."

Archibald backed slowly away from the line between Jerry and Doc. For he perceived that there was danger in the air—danger of a greater sharpness of edge than any that he had ever looked upon before.

"What questions, you little rat?"

"Am I a rat, then?"

"You're damn' right, you are."

"Jerry, I am gonna get you for that."

"I am right here, waiting. . . ."

"Then take it. . . ."

The big man, being in the direct line of Archibald's eyes, could be seen to snatch at a hip pocket and drag forth from it a gun of formidable length. But little Doc merely flicked his fingers beneath his coat, and another gun twinkled on the edge of his gesture. He fired first, and Jerry dropped his gun. He began to drop by degrees, first on sagging legs, then to his knees in the sand, and lastly he fell upon his hands.

The little man tucked away his gun with a gesture as swift as that which had brought it forth. He walked over to the edge of the verandah and said: "I had ought to put another slug in your carcass, you skunk. I hadn't ought to let you live and annoy another man the way you do me. But I'm tender-hearted, I am. Dog-gone me if I ain't a regular woman, when it comes to that."

With this quiet pronouncement, he stepped from the verandah and approached his horse. There was no haste in his movements.

By this time, Archibald was kneeling beside the wounded man, and the latter lay stretched upon his side. The hotel proprietor came to the door of his place—another door or two slammed—and footfalls were heard as men approached on the run.

"Look here, Doc," said the proprietor in a most unexclamatory manner. "I think you've killed Jerry."

"I hope I have," said Doc, "but I guess that I aimed a mite too low. But I still got a hope. He's needed killing for a long time."

"Here comes his cousin, Doc. You better slide along."

"I don't mind if I do. I guess that I've about used up my luck for this day."

"So long, Doc. Take care of yourself."

"Thanks, Smithie. I'll try. Give my regards to the sheriff and the rest of the boys."

Doc turned the head of his horse and departed, the horse jogging without haste down the road, and the little crowd came swirling around the wounded. The bungling hands of Archibald were pushed aside by the professional assurance of a doctor who examined hastily and then pronounced: "A tough one like Jerry, he'll get along all right. How you feel, Jerry?"

"I feel hit."

There was a loud and general laugh. "He's got nerve, Jerry has."

"You feel hit, all right, but have you got a sinking feeling . . . like you was losing a lot of strength and needed a rest?"

"No. I want a drink."

"Get him a drink of water."

"The devil, you know I don't mean water."

Another laugh.

"I think you'll pull through, right enough, Jerry. You just keep your head up, will you?"

"I'll need a pillow for that. Take me inside, will you? I hate havin' the sun in my eyes, this way."

They picked him up.

"What was wrong between you and Doc Aldrich. I thought that Doc and you was pals?"

"Oh, sure, we been working together pretty close to fifteen years, now. But the other day he went in and got him a suit of Sunday clothes to go to a dance. And he got trousers that was too tight. I told him that he looked like a sailor on shore leave in 'em. And he got to figuring on that and brooding on it, you know. And finally he up and give that suit of clothes to a tramp. After he give the suit away, of course he got madder and madder at me for what I had said. The other night, him and me had a few words, and he quit the job and rode into town. That was the last that I seen of him until we met up, just now. My gat, it hung in my pocket. You'll find the lining of that there pocket all tore where the sight caught into it. Otherwise, I would sure of salted the little rat. . . ."

So explained Jerry as he was carried from the sight and the hearing of Archibald into the interior of the hotel. But Archibald himself did not follow the crowd. He remained in the open air, for he was full of thought that was to the effect that flivvers and newspapers and delivery trucks had not yet vitally altered the spirit of the great West.

Chapter Six

"THE WAR STARTS"

When the evening of that same day darkened, Mr. Irving hired a horse from the livery stable and rode it east along the same road over which the lawyer had driven him that afternoon. When he came to the low outer wall of Irving Valley, he turned to the right. Presently he approached a tall gate of wrought-iron work with a stone fence running back on one side and a hedge on the other, and a newly planted woodland within. He opened the gate, and now he was riding up the well-made gravel road toward the house of Mr. Watson.

Mr. Watson built things that he hoped would outlast him, and on whatever had to do with himself, he did not care what money he had to pay out. This graveled road, for instance, was not made by the easy application of a thin layer of crushed rock, followed by a strewing of rolled gravel. Instead, the road had been excavated to a considerable depth, and in the broad trench hewn blocks of stone were laid as the first layer. Above these blocks, there were smaller but equally regular stones, and above these a layer of finer gravel—finally a surfacing almost as fine as sand. Thus in five layers this road was built, and, although it looked as simple as any other graveled road, yet Mr. Irving knew, by the sound that the feet of his horse made in the road, that there was rock beneath him. He could tell by the most cursory examination that this road was the real article guaranteed for a whole handful of centuries, just as he had known in a single glance that the pair of heavy gates that he had just opened were not part of some wholesale manufacture, but were specimens of handiwork, designed by an artist of price.

Against the moon, he had regard for the plantation of trees through which he was now riding, and the arrangement of forest and clearing. By the time he had come in view of the house, Archibald Irving recognized the handicraft of some expert landscape gardener—the same, no doubt, who had terraced the land near the house itself.

The house was disappointingly modest at first glance, after an approach so imposing. When Archibald examined it more in detail, he saw that it was better than it seemed. If it was low in stature, it was wide in expanse. It was of the Spanish type that turns blank, eyeless walls toward the exterior and reserves its grace and airy charm and all its warmth of color for the patio and the interior gardens.

When Mr. Irving tethered his horse and approached the entrance, he was preparing himself ardently for the task that lay before him. At least, that task would be simplified in a certain degree by the manifest culture of his host.

A big old man with a ruddy face and a great bulbous nose and a little pair of glittering eyes came hurrying out, holding Irving's card in his hand.

"Are you Archie Irving? I am Watson, of course. My dear boy . . . it is happiness to have you with me. It is a happiness to have dear old Ned's nephew under my roof . . . come in with me . . . this way . . . mind your step down. . . ."

Someone said that you cannot indict a whole nation, but the inverse is equally true, and, when a whole nation indicts a single man, he is apt to be in some difficulty when he casts up his final accounting. At least, so thought Archibald as he went in at the side of his host. He thought, furthermore, that even when a single country united in the solemn condemnation of one of its citizens, there was apt to be a bit of logic behind them all.

He masked these thoughts, which was not difficult, for Archibald had been presented by nature with one of those smooth, bland faces that reveal not a whit more than their owner desires to show. When Archibald smiled, no one could suspect him of double dealing. When he laughed, he shook like a jelly with his mirth.

He smiled frequently, and the first time that Mr. Watson attempted a joke, Archibald laughed so heartily that Mr. Watson leaned back in his chair and let his own mind relax. He was convinced that he was dealing with a fool—just as certainly as Mr. Vincent knew.

"But," said Archibald, when he accepted his second glass of moonshine whisky, "but, Mister Watson, I have come to see you, tonight, on a serious errand. I'd like to have a few moments of your serious attention."

"With all my heart," said Mr. Watson. "If there is anything that I can do for you . . . any advice that I can give you . . . you may call upon me to the utmost of my powers."

"It is advice . . . only advice," said young Mr. Irving, "that I would like to have from you."

Instantly the warmth of Mr. Watson became treble and even tenfold. He leaned forward with actual eagerness, his elbows on his knees, like one who is hungry for the riddle.

"My poor uncle . . . ," began Archibald, and saw a shadow like a falling curtain descend across the face of his host.

"Ah, yes, poor Ned Irving! And what of him?"

"I am sorry to say," said Archibald, "that, when my poor uncle died, he was possessed by an obsession."

"Indeed?"

"That he had been unjustly treated."

"Ah?"

The Last Irving

It was curious to see the warmth of Mr. Watson turn to coolness, the coolness to ice, and the ice to a veritable glacial chill that whole centuries of sunshine could not have penetrated.

"In fact, sir, my uncle died filled with the belief that he had been robbed, and his life work taken away from him by most thievish methods."

Mr. Watson was silent. His face had the sympathetic interest of a granite sphinx or an image in glass. Even his bulbous nose glowed less brightly.

"And the man," said Archibald, "that my uncle accused is a neighbor of yours, Mister Watson."

Twenty centuries of ice were banished from the rigid countenance of Mr. Watson.

"You astonish me, Archibald!"

"And, in fact, I have come to ask you if my uncle could possibly be right? I have come to ask for your advice in the matter?"

The final crusts of cold dissipated. Warm spring breathed in the features of Mr. Watson. "My dear boy, ask what you will of me!"

"The man my uncle accuses is named Fraser. . . ."

"Ah."

"I am a stranger in this country, of course, but I thought that you might know this man. Alexander Fraser . . . ?"

"The greatest scoundrel, my boy, that ever reached the age of seventy. The greatest villain that I have ever known. I promise you that."

"Then there may be something in what I read in my uncle's last letter."

"If it is villainy on the part of Fraser, anything is possible . . . I assure you."

"Hold on. I'll read you the extract from the letter." He

drew from his pocket a worn and wrinkled sheet of paper, covered with a very close, fine handwriting. He even held the folded paper toward Mr. Watson. "You remember my uncle's handwriting, of course?"

The smile grew rigid on the face of Mr. Watson while he perused a line or two of that sheet. What he saw, he recognized. It was the true hand of Mr. Irving, so lately dead and lamented in Irving Valley, and all the country roundabout.

The youth took from his pocket a pair of spectacles— large, round, horn-rimmed. He fitted them to his nose, and he lighted a cigarette which he smoked in a lengthy holder. He read:

And as for your own future motions in the legal profession, when I saw that I might need future time to pay, I hurried to Mr. Fraser and told him that I might have some difficulty. He told me frankly that he would be sorry to extend the loan at this particular time, because he had a particular need for that money and that the value of it would be much greater than its mere face . . . in a word, he held me up. I was very desperate, as you may judge. I knew that this was an affair in which it would be hard to interest any conservative Eastern bank, and therefore I finally offered the unconscionable money shark a bonus of ten thousand dollars cash . . . payable at once. And he took the money which I counted down into his hand. He took the money and gave me the assurance that the time would be extended . . . only, like an incredible jackass, I failed to get that assurance in writing. For the first time I tell this to you. I have been ashamed to let my lawyer know what a frightful gull. . . .

"Wait!" cried Mr. Watson. He stood still and tall before

his chair, from which he had risen, as though a hand had pulled him up.

"Do you mean to tell me . . . in the name of heaven, begin that reading again."

"He took the money which I counted down into his hand. . . ."

"Enough!" cried Watson. He still stood stiff and tall before his chair, yet it was odd that a villainy so small as this should have shocked him. "Ten thousand dollars . . . quite on the side!" he cried. "The cur . . . the unspeakable low cur!" He began to stride up and down the room. "Ten thousand! Does it not say ten thousand? Let me see the place! Ten thousand dollars . . . and for that, too . . . why, confound him, I'll make him wish that he never heard that your uncle was a gull and could be plucked. I'll make him sweat for this thing, my boy. The scoundrel. The greedy fool! The traitor!"

Mr. Watson, in an enormous rage, neglected to enforce his demand for a sight of the letter, and young Archibald hastily put the envelope away—a much rubbed and worn and pocket-soiled jacket of paper.

"I only wondered," said Archibald, "if you could advise me if such a thing were really possible. . . ."

"Possible?" cried Watson. "Yes, and probable, too! It explains many things. Let me tell you, my boy, that this man Fraser is a villain so complete that he would betray his oldest business associate for the sake of a petty profit on the side . . . he would . . . I shall let him know who I am. Advice? I tell you, young man, I shall do more than advise you. I shall fight this battle for you with my own hands!"

Chapter Seven

"MR. FRASER"

The light still burned in Mr. Fraser's office at eleven in the night. That was not an unusual occurrence, for the entire life of Mr. Fraser was circumscribed by the walls of that office. It was not a spacious chamber, but, as Mr. Fraser would have informed you at once, life is not to be known, whether for happiness or for value, by the trappings in which it is passed. Adjoining the office, there was a little sleeping closet—a chamber hardly eight by seven, with a narrow cot on one side. Here Mr. Fraser was in the habit of lying down when his night work kept him so late that there was little purpose in going to his home to sleep. He had a change of clothes, a razor, and other little necessities tucked into a corner of the sleeping closet for those nights when he remained in the bank until the next working day began.

On the whole, there was only one thing that *ever* made Mr. Fraser leave the building, and that was a subtle sense of shame. Because he knew that men always pointed him out as a miser, and he did not wish to have his passion for industry still further mistaken for the same miserly instinct. So he maintained rooms outside the bank.

It was at the side door of the bank, leading toward this private room, that young Archibald Irving tapped at this late hour of the night. All of Irvington slept. Indeed, midnight was never a waking time in the town, except for gay Saturdays.

The door opened a mere inch, and a brutal voice inquired

what Irving would have.

"I want to see old Fraser," said Archibald Irving.

"Are you known to him?" asked the voice.

"Tell him that I am Archibald Irving and ask him. . . ."

The door suddenly slammed shut. Young Archibald, fairly sure that this ended matters for that night, at the least, still stood about on one foot and then on the other, uncertain whether he had not spoiled all the complicated game that he had planned. As he shifted about, the door opened again. A dimly burning lantern showed to him a face as brutal as the voice—a broad, murderous countenance with two rat-bright eyes planted as close as possible to a turned-up nose—a prize fighter's nose. Here was a man who took pride in being dangerous and rough. He greeted Archibald with a snarl and waved the visitor in ahead of him. A chill crept into Archibald's spine as he walked in advance; he half expected to be crashed to the floor by a blow from behind at any moment.

Presently, at the end of the narrow dark hall, on which no outer windows opened, the progress of Archibald was stopped by a door.

"Knock!" commanded his guide.

Archibald knocked and a sharp voice asked: "Who's there?"

"Archibald Irving."

"Charlie, show him in."

Charlie stepped to the fore. He said with considerable smoothness and snarling viciousness: "All the time that you're in that there room, I'm out here. There ain't no way of getting out of that, without you come this way. So. . . ."

He took a key, unlocked the door, and glared at Archibald as the latter stepped through. From the eyes of the withered little man who sat behind the great desk, a message flashed toward the guard, who now closed the door softly.

"And now, young man," began Mr. Fraser, turning slowly around in his swivel chair. "And now, young man, what can I do for you?"

There was no possible source in the shriveled soul of Fraser for any amenity other than this time-honored business form.

"Don't get up," said Archibald cheerfully, as he advanced with outstretched hand. "Don't get up, sir. Because I have come for only an instant . . . a little bit of advice that I hope to beg from you. . . ."

In the first place, of course, there had not been the slightest intention on the part of the banker of rising from his place. In the second place, it was pleasant to have such intentions mistaken. In the third place, the round, plump face of jolly Mr. Irving was just the type that Mr. Fraser liked to see passing into his office—the type of the born gull. Fourthly, and most important of all—the youth had come for advice. Which meant, instantly, that he had not come to reproach or upbraid; neither could he have come to borrow. For one does not, as a rule, come to borrow cash and advice all on the very same evening.

Beyond all this, the hour was late, and men who ask for advice at midnight usually are in trouble. But men in trouble were the special diet upon which Mr. Fraser preyed. They were the meat course in the repasts he best enjoyed.

For all of these reasons, he actually smiled upon this youth in the most kindly fashion. The hired watchdog in the passageway would have gaped with surprise to behold such an expression upon the face of the ogre.

Mr. Fraser said: "Of course, I am glad to see the son of my old friend. Sit down, lad. Sit down! And tell me what's new in automobile fashions. No, we'll let that wait. Tell me, rather, what advice I can give you. It's a rare thing to find the youth of this nation willing to listen to advice, far less to seek for it from old men. Now, lad, I am glad to see you. Sit down. I'd offer you a cigar, but I make it a rule never to smoke or permit smoking in the office. . . ."

Something told Archibald Irving that it would be well not to waste time. It would be well to go at once to the point. And so he went to work.

"In the first place, it is an affair that begins with my uncle, Ned Irving. You knew him, of course, and I understand that you were connected with a loan that he secured. . . ."

The same arctic cold that had overspread the face of Mr. Watson earlier in the evening now appeared in the eyes of little Mr. Fraser.

Archibald Irving hastened to add: "My poor uncle, who it appears was not much of a businessman, held that you, Mister Fraser, were quite guiltless, but that you were forced to push home the deal because of business necessities."

A glimmer of light appeared in the dark brow of Mr. Fraser.

"But for Mister Watson, my uncle had a settled aversion. I am going to read you a selection from the last letter in which he knew that his death was near and which he wrote solemnly, in that knowledge. . . ."

The eye of Mr. Fraser was an eye like a hawk's now. It fairly burned.

"I am the last man in the world," he said, "to attribute aught good to Watson. I've seen the scandalous heart in that man's breast all of these years, as the whole country will witness. I've exposed the hypocrite and held him up to the honest light in my newspaper. Ah, if your uncle could have taken warning by the experience of others. . . ."

Just close enough to the lamp to give him plenty of light

51

and close enough, also, so that Mr. Fraser could see the script clearly without making out the words—just at this range, young Archibald Irving held the letter. Then he read aloud:

And so, my dear Archie, I wish you to know that I cannot put any real blame upon Mr. Fraser. . . .

Here Mr. Fraser broke in: "Is it written down there? Is it really written down there?"

"You can see for yourself," said Archibald, thrusting the letter in front of the old man. But before Mr. Fraser had time to adjust his vision to the fine writing, Archibald, as though intent upon his reading, drew back to his chair with the paper in his hand. He went on:

I cannot put any real blame on Mr. Fraser, but the man who must be cursed now and forever is that double fiend, Watson. . . .

Once more Mr. Fraser interrupted, clapping his hands together.

"Is it really written down there?" he cried.

"Wait," said Archie, "and you'll soon understand why!"

He continued his reading:

That double fiend, Watson, because I sent a special message to him and offered him ten thousand dollars spot cash if he could arrange to extend the time of the twenty-five thousand dollar note which he held, together with the twenty-five thousand dollar note of Mr. Fraser. Watson took the cash which I offered . . . a ten thousand dollar sum which I had to almost go to the devil in order to get. . . .

"Ha!" cried Mr. Fraser. "He got an extra ten thousand from your uncle and didn't tell. . . ."

Who it was that Watson should have told and failed to do so did not appear, for Mr. Fraser suddenly set his teeth, like one who had been on the verge of divulging an important secret. And young Irving hurried on, as though he had noticed nothing:

But I was fool enough to get merely the oral promise of Mr. Watson, whom I took a frantic trip to see. . . .

"I remember, I remember!" cried Mr. Fraser, "that your uncle made a sudden trip from town . . . and I knew it was to see Watson . . . but I thought that he missed . . . ah, that scoundrel Watson. . . ."

But when the notes became due, I went to see Watson, and the knave simply said that he had no record of having received any sum of ten thousand dollars from me. And that, my lad, was the cause of my ruin.

Archibald Irving folded the letter and restored it to his pocket. "So I have come to ask. . . ."

"My boy," said the banker, "let me have a look at that page. . . ."

"Certainly," said Archibald, and drew the letter from his pocket. But while the fingertips of the banker were already clutching it, Archibald drew it thoughtfully back and shook his head.

"There is another matter on that same page," he said sorrowfully, "which is meant for no eyes but my own. I am sorry that I cannot let you see the written words, Mister Fraser."

And he put up the letter slowly, as one who regretted. "However, what I have come to you for is your advice, Mister Fraser. I cannot let this wrong go unrighted. It is pretty well known that you understand the villainies of this Watson. Now, can you make any suggestion. . . ."

"Suggestion?" cried Fraser, clasping his hands and writhing in his chair. "Suggestion, is it? Lad, I'll do more than suggest. Let me have a chance at this . . . scoundrel . . . this robber. And come to me again in a few days."

Young Archibald Irving did not seem in an aggressive humor. He allowed himself to be shown at once from the office of the money-maker. He bade the scowling guard a cheerful good night and wandered whistling back toward the hotel. When he got to it, he found a half a dozen men in the act of mounting their horses at the hitching rack. He heard the news—Doc Aldrich, who had shot Jerry Swinton, had been chased and missed by the first posse, had stolen a horse to help him on his way, and now a new detachment of men was riding out to try to catch him.

Chapter Eight

"HIS MASTER'S VOICE"

Let us leave the chronicling of the deeds—or rather the absence of deeds—in the career of Mr. Irving and turn to other matters, just as Irvington turned, at about this time. There had been a great thrill of excitement at first. People were hungry for a glimpse of the last of the great fighting line of the Irvings, the frontiersmen, ranchers, and financiers. But after the major had had him to lunch, and the people of the town—merchants and ranchers—had had a chance to examine his mild eye and his plump, easy-going face, there was a general falling off in interest.

For it was decided at once that mentally as well as physically this young man was a far, far cry from the vigorous race of the earlier Irvings who had made such great chunks of history in that vicinity. They began to look upon Archibald as belonging to that large group of men who are more to be smiled upon than respected.

Ordinarily, this would have made him well enough liked. But it was considered that mere good humor was such a falling off from the qualities that were expected of an Irving, that a general sneer began to be directed at this smiling youth.

However, he seemed oblivious to it, as he was oblivious of all that was unpleasant. The vigor of his apathetic calm—if one could use such a paradoxical phrase—overbore all that threatened his happiness. Money itself seemed to make no difference to him.

While it was wondered how this scion of a ruined race would take vengeance upon those who had brought about its downfall, it was reported and currently believed that young Archibald was busying himself buying a new equipment of aluminum kitchen ware through a traveling salesman who had interested him in its durable properties. Irvington shook its hardy head and sneered again.

In two breasts, however, Archibald had planted something more than smiles and contemptuous sneers. Not that they felt less contempt, but that they felt the greater wrath. Rage burned unceasingly in the old and robust breast of Mr. Watson, and in the old and withered chest of Mr. Fraser.

A note came to Mr. Fraser in the morning mail:

Dear Sandy:
I must see you at once. Business of the greatest importance. Can you drive up the valley this morning and we'll have a chance for a chat?

As ever yours,
W.

Mr. Fraser had already dispatched a note on his own behalf to Watson, saying:

I am going to be in the valley road this morning, early. You had better come along. I know something that you will be glad to hear.

Fraser

Now he sent off another note, saying that he would be in the valley at ten and expected to find Watson there.

What delayed Fraser so long was the little matter of Mrs. Aldrich and her farm. Since the flight of Doc from Irvington after the shooting of Jerry Swinton, Mrs. Aldrich had given up all hope and decided that she would leave that part of the country. For seven long years, now, she had struggled to keep the little farm going; Doc had helped her valiantly. He worked his hands to the bone for six months of the year, doing nine-tenths of the work around the place. In the other six months of the year, he spent his time in laboring for hard cash for others. In this way, they had made a good deal of progress, and, while they had continued to pay a fat seven percent to Mr. Fraser, they had whittled off the corners of the mortgage and brought it down to a very much more reasonable sum than it had been at the time of the death of the elder Aldrich.

Now that Mrs. Aldrich wanted to move, however, she found that the little farm had, in the eyes of Fraser, apparently, a value that was only a third of that which she had expected. And this morning, with her bony, work-distorted hands clasped in her lap and her weary eyes centered upon his face, she listened while the expert pencil of the banker went swiftly down the list that she had prepared: "Cows . . . good. Valuable, if you can find anybody to milk them. But where do you find that around here? Where do you find it, when they want beef cattle and are willing to use condensed milk? Plows . . . all ten years old and worn out. . . ."

"Oh, plenty, plenty good enough to do all the work that a body could ask of them for another ten years!"

"Don't tell me, Missus Aldrich. I've attended too many sales. The value I can put on your farm is just what it would bring in the market. What *you* can make out of it with your labor and your sons . . . that is important to you. What *I* can make out of it is the thing that is important to me. I don't like to talk brusquely to you. But this is business. And business is business. You don't want me to *give* you money, do you?"

Oh, no, she would rather starve than receive charity. She would far rather starve!

Poor Mrs. Aldrich. Before he finished his half hour talk with her, he had beaten down an eight thousand dollar farm with a two thousand dollar mortgage to such a degree that the poor old woman was willing to take two thousand cash and the cancellation of the mortgage in payment.

That was good business. Mr. Fraser knew that he could sell that farm in ten days for double what the widow got from him. As he buttoned up his old, threadbare, motoring coat after the interview, his heart and his very stomach were warmed, as though that four thousand dollars in profit had already been eaten by him, and now was being digested and added to the stores of his wealth.

Sometimes it seemed to Mr. Fraser that his money was a sensible part of his flesh. The interest from good investments was the circulation of his blood; the growth of his fortune was the growth of himself. So that he was ever a young and growing boy. That was why the eyes of other old men grew filmed and dull, but his eye retained the brightness and quickness of a four thousand dollar profit.

Then he went forth to his garage.

It has already been mentioned that an automobile was the one extravagance—even the one pleasure—that Mr. Fraser enjoyed outside of business itself. He loved a fine car with a redoubled passion.

His business was housed in a shack, his home—a mere hovel, yet the garage was a fine, new building of stoutest concrete, roomy, and complete to the latest details. There was a trench in the floor where a mechanic could descend and work the inwards of the car from beneath. There were electric lights on long cords, tools beyond listing, well-nigh. In the rear of this garage, or rather opening as a wing of it, was fitted up a complete little blacksmith shop, with a forge and an electric bellows. If some little job of soldering needed to be done, the mechanic could attend to it.

In this garage there reigned as a sort of tributary prince—almost independent of Mr. Fraser—almost a king, a chauffeur who was also a master mechanic. To this greasy genius, Mr. Fraser was in the habit of bowing for advice. This great man was consulted by the banker in the feverish hours of joy, trembling hope, and despair that preceded the purchase of a new car. Once, five years before, a car that Mr. Fraser had bought contrary to the advice of this mechanic had developed mysterious ailments. The engine had not operated properly. It had coughed, weakened, and stopped upon the level road. But although Mr. Fraser knew that his mechanic must probably have tampered with the fine car, yet he dared not complain. Because ordinarily and when taking care of a car on whose purchase price he had probably received a commission from the agent, the mechanic was, beyond all doubt, an unsurpassed genius.

Sometimes, for half an hour at a stretch, the banker sat awed and silent, watching the strong, learned fingers of the mechanic at work in the garage. At those times Mr. Fraser dared not speak. Once a bit of advice from him had caused the laborer to leap to his feet with strong and strange curses, rush toward his rooms to pack his grip and depart. All the way to the station, Mr. Fraser had followed him, entreating. At length the genius was persuaded by the banker to return.

Yet again, a few words from Mr. Fraser had caused a great monkey wrench to fly on wings through the air straight at his head. He had ducked just in time to have his hat carried off his head and through the windowpanes with a crash. But he dared not protest. He paid for the broken window and crept away in silence.

For this mechanic *was* a genius. In vain, in vain did the stupid Watson attempt to duplicate the beautiful automobiles of Mr. Fraser. For the first month, they might do well enough, but at the end of that time their engines would begin to whisper and then to wheeze—if ever so slightly. Whereas the automobiles of Fraser were ever ready and ever running like the smoothest oiled silk.

On this morning, the dignitary of the garage had just descended from his chambers above, with mid-morning tea still moist upon his lips. He answered the greeting of Mr. Fraser with a cold and distant nod, and then, having paused to fill his pipe and light the same, he slid back the garage door upon its well-oiled hinges—a silent, perfect door.

Mr. Fraser paused in the doorway. Before him stood two sleekly shimmering monsters. The one was of darkest, richest maroon; the other was glorious deep blue. Which was the better car? It would be hard to tell. English craft had made the one honestly and well; German craft had put the other together with a cunning precision, like a delicate watch. Toward the blue car Mr. Fraser moved. He cast a frightened glance at the god of the region and then opened the door. He was about to settle himself in the driver's seat, when a calm voice said: "The other car this morning. . . ."

"Surely," said Mr. Fraser prayerfully, "nothing has gone wrong with . . . ?"

"I've said my piece," said the deity in overalls. "You better take the other car." He turned his back and folded his arms.

Mr. Fraser took the other car.

Chapter Nine

"THUNDER AND LIGHTNING"

The instant that he touched the self-starter and the engine came to life, nine-tenths of his regrets fell from him. He paused, with the clutch out, and listened. It was barely audible—a subdued and distant murmur, but a murmur of boundless strength. And was there a vibration?

To nerves less sensitive than those of Mr. Fraser, there would have been none, but to him there came the faintest thrill—like the stir of a tiny current of electricity over the wire and against the skin, just noisy enough, just rough enough to make its existence known. What more could one ask of an automobile?

Mr. Fraser was content. He pressed the accelerator.

"*Don't* race your engine," said the tired voice of the god at the garage door.

For the hundredth time he said it, and Mr. Fraser shrank small inside his coat collar. He dropped in the gearshift lever, touching it with a delicate forefinger—the clutch came gently in, and the great car nosed its way out onto the road.

When he went from first to second, on leaving the garage, Mr. Fraser always shuddered lest the mechanic should hear a noise. And because he was so tensed with terror, he was always sure to make the gears clash a little. Then, turning his frightened head, he was sure to see the calm, scornful smile of the great man in the door of the garage.

Sometimes that smile would make Mr. Fraser unhappy for

61

half a day, and often he dreamed at night of making a perfect, noiseless shift from high to third on a fast hill, and saw the mechanic sit suddenly erect in the seat, filled with the wonder and silence of true applause. Or he dreamed of learning some mystery of the car's engine and, when the great man went wrong, of pointing it out to him, calmly, without pride, but as one who knew. For such a moment, sometimes Mr. Fraser felt that he would pay as much as half of his fortune.

On this morning, as usual, the change to second was made with a slight grating noise, and Mr. Fraser was so angered and so frightened at once that he forgot all about any further nervousness and made the next two gear shifts perfectly. Then, with oiled smoothness, the car fled down the open road. Before him a stranger's automobile appeared—a stranger's, for Mr. Fraser knew by heart every license plate in the county. No difficult task to that head of his and its stock of figures of all kinds. The specially constructed siren in the Fraser car shrieked, the big machine leaped past, a maroon streak of beauty, and Mr. Fraser swerved it closely in front of the stranger. He loved doing that. The curses from the other car never troubled his conscience any more than the curses from a heartbroken debtor.

He hit the long climb of the Irvington Hill at such a speed that he did not have to drop into fourth until he was almost at the summit. Then he went whooping over the top in such high spirits that he almost forgot all that brought him forth on this morning until, in the valley road before him, he saw the rear of a blue machine swing out of view around a curve. It was Watson. No other car—saving his own—was cut so low, and with such serpentine grace—no other car in all the county.

So Mr. Fraser fed the maroon beauty to sixty miles an hour and leaped down the valley with the horn screaming.

Ahead of him, the blue car hastened, but not fast enough. The heart of Mr. Fraser exulted in his cramped breast.

It was all very well that Mr. Watson was brave when he sat on a horse's back or when he confronted men. Perhaps such a share of courage had not been poured hot into the breast of Fraser. But when he sat behind the wheel of an automobile, fear left him. Only joy and pride in the speed that responded to the pressure of his foot remained to him.

Now, with the tail of his eye, he watched the needle of the speedometer waver to sixty-one—three—four—five—

"Give up, you coward!" screamed Mr. Fraser to the shrieking blast that combed around his windshield.

The big blue car lounged to the side of the road, and the maroon dashed past, with the accelerator still depressing, the speedometer still rising—and Mr. Fraser sitting back against the great soft cushion, looking straight before him, blandly impervious to the existence of the other.

He was so pleased with himself for this performance that, as he let the car run on more slowly and finally sent it to the side down a narrow lane—their usual meeting place—he still found it hard to gather the proper violence of anger in his breast.

He got out from the car where it stopped, and was walking up and down as the blue machine drew up beside him. And— "Good morning, Billy."—he said to Watson.

Mr. Watson, with a savage scowl, drew from his huge and ancient hand the driver's glove, but answer returned he none, except that blasting glare.

And Mr. Fraser, with the acid running into his brain as he remembered all that he had heard from young Irving, said with an evil smile: "I've asked you out to talk to you about the unwritten laws of partnerships, Billy."

"Sandy," said the other with thunder in his voice, "I've

come to talk to you about the same thing."

"Ah," said Fraser, "it's the first time in thirty years that we've begun by agreeing with each other. Maybe, Billy, we won't *separate* with an agreement."

"It depends," said Watson, "on the thickness of your skin. But I think that I'll reach you, tough as you are."

"In the first place," said Alexander Fraser, "when we started to work together, we agreed that there was a need for absolute honesty . . . with each other. Did we not?"

"We did," nodded Watson. And he licked his lips. "You're preparing my own ground for me, Sandy. I cannot help warning you of that!"

"Bah!" exclaimed Fraser. "We were to act hand in glove whenever a big thing came along and *never* try competition . . . because we both knew that competition puts down prices, whether in a hotel or a lumberyard, or in bidding on property at a forced sale. We knew that, and we knew that, outside of each other, there was nobody in the county that was able to give us a run for our money. So we made an unwritten agreement . . . we formed a silent trust . . . and we masked that trust by pretending to hate each other."

Watson nodded, his eyes burning.

"I have written out the very lies about myself that you've published in your fool paper, Sandy," said Watson. "And you've done the same by me. And I tell you, man, that crooked as I know you are. . . ."

There was a yell of rage from Fraser, but the larger man went on: "Crooked as a snake, or worse than a snake, yes. But I really thought, all these years, that you were playing square with me. Not because you respected me or loved me. No, damn you, because there's no love in you for anything in the world except a thing of steel and wood like that car you drive . . . but I thought that you wouldn't dare to double-cross me, for the simple reason that you never knew what money-making *was* until I showed you how we could take this county by the throat and bleed it white for our mutual benefit. I thought you were making too much money to even *dream* of crookedness. . . ."

Another hoarse cry came from Mr. Fraser. For it suddenly occurred to him that the very thunder that had been prepared in his hand for the blasting of his enemy was now being cast at his own head. It was a species of unfairness, obviously, and it maddened the good Fraser.

"Will you stop?" he yelled. "Will you stop your lying . . . you that were a petty land stealer, till I showed you what *business* could do . . . will you stop your lying and listen to me one half minute?"

"I'll stop a minute," said Watson. "I'm in no hurry. I *need* time to tell you what I think of you. Because I'm going to make you *crawl* before I leave you."

"Bill Watson, name a single sum of money that I ever cheated you out of?"

"I'll name one," said Watson. "A small one, too. Considering that I've meant millions to you, a sum so small that it shows that you still have the same soul of a pickpocket with which you were born. Sandy, I've made you rich . . . and yet you would lie to me and cheat me for a scoundrelly ten thousand dollars!"

The savage anger that had been rising in the breast of Mr. Fraser had come to the boiling point. But there was a fuel of satisfaction feeding the flame, in that he felt he could dull the edge of Watson's accusation, whatever it might be, by producing the black evidence of young Archibald's letter against his partner under the rose. Here was an accusation thrown at his own head, and in almost the very same amount.

Mr. Fraser, for an instant, was silent with indignation.

And with amazement, too. He had committed plenty of small crimes against that partnership of silence and cunning in which he worked with Mr. Watson. But all of them rolled together never reached the sum of ten thousand dollars. And he knew, as he stood there, that his silence was being taken for the confession of guilt. He knew that the wrath that made his cheek pale seemed the pallor of the coward who is caught. All of which knowledge merely served to increase his fury.

He heard Watson saying calmly: "I won't say that I'll go as far as to refuse to forgive you, Sandy. Pay back to me my share of the ten thousand that you took in. Pay me the five thousand, and I'll forgive you the interest. It's not the money that grieves me, but the lack of faith in you. Pay me the money, and, without any more ado, we'll be friends once more."

Here the rage of Sandy Fraser at last turned into words. He screamed and clenched his fists. "Bill Watson, how can such a lie come out of a man? It needs a big man like you to tell such a lie. It would break the throat of a little man!"

"Do I lie?" said Watson. "Now, Fraser, mind you that I'm a calm man, but now you irritate me a little. However, I'll hear your talk. What is it?"

"You knew," shouted Fraser, "or you guessed why I wanted to see you here, and so you coined some lie to tell me . . . you knew that *you'd* be accused. And so you thought that you'd accuse me first."

"Oh," said the big man, sneering. "*I'm* to be accused, then? Of what, pray?"

"Of the very sum you've named! You've taken in ten thousand dollars, Watson. And five thousand belongs to me. I'll take your check for that sum this morning."

Chapter Ten

"MIGHT OVER RIGHT"

A wild exclamation formed upon the lips of Watson. Upon second thought, he swallowed his first impulse and walked a pace or two in silence.

"Does your guilt gag you?" yelled Sandy Fraser.

"Guilt?" howled Watson.

Then he broke into a sneering laughter and continued his pacing up and down, his face black with thought. In the vigor of that pacing, he swept back and forth between two shrubs, and each time he approached one of them, a figure among the bushes crouched lower. For here was innocent Archibald Irving, whose morning stroll had carried him far, far out of Irvington, and over the hill, and down into Irving Valley, and even to the very same spot, where he had seen the two blue cars halted, where the telescope had betrayed to him the two financiers, walking arm in arm. Now, he drank in their talk with avidity. Only one thing threatened to betray him, and that was a frame-shaking laughter that fairly made his ribs ache in the effort to choke it back.

"Guilty?" continued big Watson, his red nose now burning like a candle's flame. "Oh, Fraser, in pity for yourself don't go on with this talk. In shame, man, don't grovel so low."

Fraser struck his hands together and leaped a few inches into the air, which was as far as his weak legs would propel him. "Watson, Watson," he yelled. "Are you to talk of shame to me? You miser! You scheming, money-loving knave! You . . . you. . . . Oh, Watson, don't dream that you're in your office now, with a poor, miserable bankrupt begging off his time of payment. You're talking to a man that knows you and reads you like an open book . . . a man who sees through you and despises what he sees. Do you understand me? And you're not going to overbear me. I'll not leave this spot until I have in my pocket your check. . . ."

"Silence!" shouted Watson.

The vigor of his roar and the fury of his face swept some of the rising color out of the face of withered Fraser.

Watson approached with enormous strides. He towered over the smaller man. "Fraser, you lie, and you know that you lie. I want to be calm, and I want to be fair. I tell you, I understand. It was only the gold fever that did the dirty trick. It was not really you. It was just the gold fever, which upset your wits and would not let you see that by taking a little secret profit like that you were really harming yourself! But what I want first of all from you is simply an admission that you were wrong. Will you admit it?"

And Mr. Fraser like a snarling cat answered: "I'll see you. . . ."

He answered upon impulse, and so did Mr. Watson. Except that the answer of Mr. Watson took a more physical form than mere speech. His right fist shot forward and clipped Mr. Fraser along the side of the head and dropped him to the ground.

He was not really hurt, however. It was rather shock, indeed, that had floored him. Now he started to struggle to his feet, crying: "I'll make you groan for this, Watson. I'll make you wish to heaven. . . ."

But the blow that Watson struck had merely served to arouse the larger man. All the brute in him that was ordinarily expended through the machinations of his business interests now saw an opportunity to loose itself in physical violence. He ran in and caught little Fraser by the nape of the neck and, mouthing meaningless words of fury, began to drag the smaller man about and whack him with clumsy, roundabout blows. Sometimes it was the soft palm of his hand that struck Fraser; sometimes it was his wrist. Only now and then his knuckles got in a glancing blow.

Fraser was not badly hurt. He was terrified to the verge of death by this violent passion. He was not accustomed to being met by anything but humility and courtesy, to say the least. It was a stunned instant before he could realize what was happening, and then he shrieked loudly for help. "Murder!" screamed Fraser.

Watson's big hand fumbled for the neck of his partner and closed that screech to a mumble.

"Why don't I finish you off now?" said Watson through teeth set with gratified force. "Why don't I finish you now? You rat! You rat!"

Mr. Fraser curled up in a ball and wrapped his face and throat in his skinny arms. "Mercy, Billy!" he pleaded. "For pity's sake . . . don't kill me. You'll lose money by it. You'll lose money . . . beat me, Bill, but don't kill me!"

Mr. Watson stopped the beating, but the exercise and the morning air and the venting of a dislike that he had felt for many years were all so agreeable to him that he now marched up and down breathing hard and spouting out disconnected phrases.

"Stand up to me! Little viper! You've needed it for a long time. Little fool . . . I'll teach you!"

He was like a bully in a schoolyard, which, in fact, he had once been. Like the typical bully, after his victory he felt no shame because of the difference between his size and that of his opponent. He was merely satisfied.

Once or twice, Fraser began to move cautiously toward a semi-direct position, but the instant he uncurled, a stamping step and a snarl from Watson made him curl up again, with a whine for mercy. Watson, each time, smiled with gratified superiority.

"Very well," said Watson finally, "all that I'll do is to take your check for ten thousand on the spot!"

"I . . . *ten* thousand . . . ?" said Fraser. "Man, man, even if I *did* take ten thousand, only half would be due. . . ."

"Will you try your bargaining talent on *me?*" yelled Mr. Watson.

"No!" gasped out Mr. Fraser. And yet he could not help adding: "But I haven't a checkbook with me, Watson."

It was a foolish speech. Mr. Watson had known his companion too many years to be in doubt upon such a point as this. His strong hand was instantly in one of his victim's pockets, and he jerked forth the checkbook and threw it in Fraser's face.

"You poor, sniveling cur!" said Watson. "Now write that check!"

And Mr. Fraser wrote it. He lingered out each detail in the unhappy business. He first had a hard time making his fountain pen flow. And then he was ignorant of the date.

"Shall I make it to cash or to you, Billy?"

"Cash," said Watson scornfully. "I'm well enough known, I suppose, to get that check cashed when I present it."

At last, the faltering pen of Mr. Fraser wrote out the check in full.

He waved it in the air until it was dried, and then presented it to the conqueror.

Mr. Watson folded it across, and scribbled his name on the back. Then he placed it carefully in his wallet, and the wallet in his pocket. And after the wallet was stowed, he patted his coat with a fond gesture.

"Not a bad profit for a single morning's work," he said. "Not a bad profit at all, Sandy. And though I suppose you are a little irritated, just now, I'm afraid that I shall have to irritate you still further by letting you know that I really don't give a hang whether you wish to break away from our partnership or not. I've been ashamed of associating with you for a long time. However, before I leave you, I'd like to know how you had the effrontery, Fraser . . . the infernal, absurd effrontery to accuse me of having taken ten thousand dollars away from you. If I had pinned you down, Fraser, what sort of testimony would you have brought up against me?"

The lips of Mr. Fraser parted to answer—and the plump-faced man in the bush quivered with excitement. Here was the point, it seemed, at which his clever and tenuous little scheme was to be broken to bits.

But no, Mr. Fraser did not speak. He examined the cold eyes of Mr. Watson and told himself that the bigger man was simply attempting to draw from his victim a statement that would serve him as an excuse for bursting into another brutal passion.

Mr. Fraser's bones already ached from the thumping that he had received. So he decided that he would not risk another verbal encounter that might so easily lead on to a matter of fisticuffs. He closed his thin mouth and, saying not a word, climbed slowly to the side like a fox.

When the pressure gauge showed two pounds, he touched the self-starter—the engine responded with a deep voice-like hum, and then, with the gear engaged and the car ready to leap away, he turned in the seat. A green devil was in his eyes, and Mr. Watson smiled as he saw the outburst about to come.

"I'll have the heart out of you for this morning's business," said Mr. Alexander Fraser. "If there's knife or gun or . . . poison in the world, I'll be after you until I have laid you . . . dead, Watson. Dead!"

The superior smile faded from the lips of Mr. Watson. In spite of himself he turned pale. For he had been thinking of cuts in the business world, and he had been comforting himself with the assurance that he was so well fortified that he could stand four-square to any blows in that field. However, death had not occurred to him. Not guns—not poison! Now it flashed through his mind that the lean-faced devil in the little man would turn to exactly those weapons and no others. Certainly the heart in the breast of Mr. Watson grew colder and colder.

The maroon-colored automobile leaped down the valley, and Mr. Watson stood staring after it with a startled countenance. He reached automatically to his hip pocket and touched the handles of an emergency revolver that he always carried with him. Had there been a reason, then, for using that gun in this very scene?

Far away, the maroon streak vanished around a curve, and just then it seemed to Mr. Watson that a stealthy hand had glided up under the tail of his coat, and that his revolver was being gently withdrawn from his pocket.

Chapter Eleven

"TABLES TURNED"

Such a thing, of course, could not be. But after a fraction of a second, Mr. Watson turned with a start—and found himself facing a young man who held in his hand the very gun that he had just removed from the trousers of Mr. Watson himself. The youth was the simple and plump-faced Archibald Irving!

Mr. Watson found himself without words for the first time in his life; then the youth tossed the revolver to the ground behind him.

"Excuse me, Mister Watson," he said, "for coming on you by surprise in this way. But it occurred to me . . . as a way of calling your attention to me . . . to take the gun out of your pocket, you know . . . because I guessed that you had one there." He seemed to find something so amusing in this foolish speech that he burst into the heartiest laughter.

"Young man," said the rich man, "I don't know what can have addled your wits, but. . . ."

"The sight of Fraser wriggling on the ground," said Archibald. "That is what has tickled me so much." And he laughed again so gaily that he could barely control himself sufficiently to add: "Because, although you had promised to fight my battle for me, it never occurred tome that you would use your fists. However, now that you have the ten thousand, I'll be very glad to have it. Very glad!"

"Zounds, boy," cried Mr. Watson. "Do you mean to say that you are robbing me?"

"Oh, dear, no," said Archibald Irving. "Robbing you? Certainly not! But I knew that you wanted the money just because it had been extorted by old Fraser by fraud from my poor, simple uncle. And I know, Mister Watson, that you would never dream of defrauding his simple nephew in a worse manner. You would never dream of that. The check is mine, of course."

Mr. Watson regarded him very soberly. "I cannot make it out," he said at length. "You have more than ten thousand dollars in your property. You are not really going to commit a crime that will outlaw you for the sake of this check of mine?"

"Outlaw me?" exclaimed Archibald. "Outlaw me?" He held up both his hands, and he rolled up his eyes, in the fervency of his protest. "I should never do a thing that might outlaw me. I don't intend to cash the check, of course."

"You don't? Then, pray, what earthly good will it do you, Archibald Irving?"

"It will act, you might say, as a rein pulling on a curb, or rather . . . it is both check and curb in one. With it I hope to control a very mettlesome horse . . . yourself."

Mr. Watson started and then burst out: "You preposterous young jackass! If you think. . . ."

"I do not think. I *know,*" said Archibald. "And there's a great difference in that. I *know* that I have you in my pocket. And I shall sell this check back to you only upon the receipt from you of a deed to all the lands of my uncle that you took from him. Every one of them, Mister Watson! Oh, yes. Every item of the profit that you made upon that transaction of partnership . . . secret partnership, I may call it."

Mr. Watson estimated the size of his opponent, and then tensed his striking muscles. He had just been using them, and he had enjoyed the exercise immensely. There lay the revolver, at a safe distance. To be sure, he was old, but he had an advantage of some fifty pounds in weight—and one never could tell.

"You young ruffian," said Mr. Watson. "You unspeakable young cad and blackguard. I do almost believe that you're really in earnest, and if you are, I will. . . ."

He advanced a full and threatening stride, but as he came to the end of it he heard Archibald Irving say: "Very good, Mister Watson. Very good! I admire courage, but I hate to see a man make a fool of himself. Now, I don't want to have to strike you. I hate violence to one's elders. But if I *do* have to use my hands on you, I'll hit you within a very few pounds of as hard as Mister Fraser could wish to turn the trick himself. *All* of me is not fat, you understand?"

He smiled most jovially at Mr. Watson, and the tall old man wavered and looked down into the beaming face, and understood that he was beaten.

"It is to be blackmail," he said suddenly.

"You may call it that," said Archibald thoughtfully. "Yes, I don't think that I can find a better title for it, offhand. Blackmail . . . yes! It gives a relish to everything . . . for some foolish reason. I feel delighted with myself. Blackmailer! Mister Watson, I am contented. It is to be blackmail."

"I deliver to you a deed to my quarter of Irving Valley," went on Watson, keeping a strong control over himself, "or else you let Mister Fraser know that you are willing to appear as a witness against me in a lawsuit. . . ."

"Precisely! You make it all so easy for me, Mister Watson . . . that it is really a pleasure to rob you. So kindly give me the check." He raised his voice a little as he said this.

Mr. Watson slowly drew out the wallet, produced the precious check, and passed it to young Archibald. As he did so, he smiled sourly.

"You young fool!" he exclaimed. "Do you think that the

mere extortion of a written check is enough to constitute blackmail on my part at the expense of Fraser? Don't you suppose that I can convince any judge that it was merely a little practical joke and that I didn't. . . ."

"A *very* practical joke," nodded Archibald. "And the judge will be pleased to learn how Fraser screamed for mercy. . . ."

"Ah, well," said Watson. "There may be something in what you say."

"Besides, Watson, such affairs are not very thoroughly appreciated in this country, and if the people ever suspected what you are, they might raise a little mob. . . ."

"Bah! I have heard such talk before. Maybe in the old days. But the automobile has brought law too close to the heels of the lazy rascals. They know better than to take any liberty in their actions in these times!"

"I cannot convince you, then? Well, I think you may stub your toe on these same Westerners, one of these days. Because they seem to me just as hardy in flivvers as they ever were in buckboards. Thank you for the check, Mister Watson."

"And what else will you have?"

"At your leisure, I shall have the deed to that land. For which I now pay you in advance . . . this brand new dollar?"

He tossed a folded dollar bill to Watson, but the latter, turning a dark crimson, allowed the money to fall unheeded to the ground.

"You may mail the deed to me . . . no, better still, you can send it by messenger. You will have time to see a lawyer and have the deed drawn up There is the value received, lying at your feet. I shall expect to have the deed in my hands by two o'clock tomorrow afternoon, or else I carry this check and the story concerning it to the afternoon paper . . . I believe that Mister Fraser controls that paper?"

The Last Irving

Mr. Watson slowly bowed his head. He had been trying to estimate just what damage the publication of that check would do to him, and finally he decided that the boy was right. Even by as small a cable as this, he had Mr. Watson tied hand and foot, and there was no escape for the older and wiser man.

"Good morning, Mister Watson."

Young Archibald Irving turned and sauntered away. The fallen revolver lay in his path. He kicked it skillfully over the top of the shrubbery and out of sight. Then he went whistling on his way, not too briskly, but walking as one who enjoyed scenery more than exercise.

"And I thought," murmured Mr. Watson, "that he was a soft-headed young fool. I thought that."

He turned up his eyes as though to call heaven to witness that such had been his very thought. Then he stooped and picked up the neglected dollar bill. This, no doubt, was the effect of an absent mind. He folded it with care, and stored it in his wallet. Then he went back to his automobile. Sitting in the driver's seat, he allowed his eyes to run caressingly over his quarter of the valley. It was all in sight. A great wedge of that valley, its nose lying blunt against the lake that was to supply with water the splendid pumping plants of Mr. Irving. . . .

Mr. Watson shook his head and sighed. It was too bad to see all of this slipping through his fingers. But long ago he had decided that finance was a gambler's game and that one must learn to take all losses with the philosophical calm of the real gamester. Here was a pretty severe tug at the strings of his purse. But after he had twisted his mouth into a severe contortion or two, he lighted a cigarette, started his car, and drove it thoughtfully up the lane, turned it, and sent it downhill again.

He saw young Archibald Irving standing by the side of the road, resting his hand upon his walking stick. Young Archibald waved and nodded with the brightest and most dispassionate of smiles.

And Mr. Watson put his foot on the brake, so that the car slowed, with the faintest of groans.

"Look here, my son, you'd better ride to town with me."

Mr. Irving replied: "You're ten thousand times kinder than I deserve. But I really like this spot very well. I think I'll stroll along and see what I can see."

Mr. Watson released the brakes, grinned broadly, and let the car roll on. The simplicity of the youth was much, much deeper than its surface valuation.

As for Archibald, he walked on through the valley until he came to a small clump of trees, and here he decided that he would sit down in the shade, since the morning sun stood high and hot in the heavens.

He advanced a step or two past the margin of the wood, when he heard something stir before him, and, looking sharply up, he had a very fine view of the round, black mouth of a .45 caliber Colt held in a firm hand. Behind the gun and the thin, strong hand there was the meager face of Doc Aldrich.

"Well, well," said young Archibald, "of all the men in the town, *I'm* the lucky one."

"Stick up your hands, kid," advised Doc Aldrich.

"Sure," remarked Archibald pleasantly, "any little thing. You don't seem to have grown much thinner, though, since I saw you last."

"Just stow that yap," said Doc unkindly. "Talking bothers me while I got thinking to do."

And he began to do his thinking with the tips of his fingers, running them through the clothes of his victim.

Chapter Twelve

"PRIVATE FIREWORKS"

With his plump arms extended above his head, Mr. Irving said: "Have you got everything?"

"You leave that to me!"

"But my arms are aching. There's a little automatic just under the pit of my left arm. You'd better take that while you're about it."

There was a grunt from Mr. Aldrich. He reached in and drew forth from the described position a gun not much larger or thicker than a cigarette case—but with a black muzzle that seemed to mean business, decidedly.

"Now, if you don't mind taking the point of that Colt from the pit of my stomach," suggested Archibald.

"Look here, kid," said Doc Aldrich, "you're full of gab, but them that pack *this* kind of guns ain't to be fooled with, and I know it. A big bow-wow gun like the one I pack, why, it's a kind of honest way of dying. But a sneakin' little pinch of poison like this here . . . no, you may be an Irving, and you may look like a simp, but you sit down there and turn your back to me while I go through your stuff. And don't you forget. I'm a hoss thief, now. And so I might as well be a murderer on top of it."

With this dour warning, he made Archibald turn his back and sit down, after which Doc Aldrich placed himself in a cross-legged position and began to go through his loot.

He maintained a little monologue as he did this: "I never

took to blondes, none."

"She's the sister of a college friend of mine," said Mr. Irving. "I carry her around with me to get used to her crooked smile and. . . ."

"Will you shut up? I need silence, while I'm thinking!" And Doc Aldrich resumed, aloud: "Forty-two bucks! For an Irving! Why, it's hardly worth taking!"

"I hear that Jerry Swinton is doing pretty fine," said Archibald.

"Yeh. That's fine, ain't it? I done a lot of worrying about that big fool, for a while. Damn him, though, I aimed to kill him, that day. He'd riled me so. Now you shut up your talk and lemme think."

He continued: "Hello . . . what's this here? Ten thous . . . holy mackerel! Ten thousand berries is promised by Mister Fraser to . . . why, damn my eyes, I never seen such a thing. Ten-thousand iron men is the medicine that old Doctor Fraser prescribes for Mister Watson. Him that he hates so bad! Ten thousand! It'll about soak up all of the profit that he'll make out of skinning ma! Ten thousand . . . but look here, mister man, how come that Watson puts his name on the back of a check and then hands it to you? Are you maybe his office boy? Shut up and don't answer. I just want to think. . . ."

"You could think all day," said Archibald, "and you'd never guess. You see. . . ."

"You poor sap . . . turn around, will you?"

But Archibald persisted in turning and even in rising to one knee, although with a guileless smile. "I want to explain," said Archibald, "that. . . ."

"Explain the devil!" exclaimed Mr. Aldrich. "I want your back turned, or. . . ."

"Hey?" yelled Archibald.

"You bonehead, will you turn around?"

"I'll be good!" cried Archibald. "But keep that gun finger of yours away from the trigger of that gat. Because there are five little chunks of lead in there all labeled . . . 'home and mother!' And they touch off with one squeeze of the hand."

"Do they?" murmured Doc in admiration. "Oh, I guessed that it was a little pet, all right. All in one squeeze? I would admire to see what they would do to a gent." And he lowered his own gun to the ground and stood up with the automatic, looking for a target.

"They would cut a man right in two," said Archibald, stepping forward conversationally. "I'll show you."

"Look here," said Doc, "will you stand back, young fool? I don't aim to do you no harm. I got to have a little cash, and I guess that you can spare yours about as well as most men that ain't worked for what they've got. But if you press me too close . . . I'll use your own gun on you."

He barked this last as Archibald answered: "You see that I've got my arms raised, don't you?" And still Archibald drifted closer.

"I see a plenty," said Doc. "But what I want is distance." And he yelled: "Keep back, or . . . !" He added: "Why, you're *crazy!*" Take it, then." And he pressed the fatal trigger. Five reports rang out upon the air, so quickly that they tripped upon the heels of one another. Before Mr. Archibald Irving could take two full steps forward, those five shots had crackled, and each at point-blank range.

Mr. Aldrich, his face twisted in ardent dislike of the work that he was doing, expected to see the last of the Irvings drop to the ground, but Archibald did not drop.

Instead, he swiftly crossed the scant half stride that separated him from the muscular body of Doc Aldrich. Just as the last echo barked back at them in a roar from the trees, a neatly compact fist landed beside the point of the jaw of Doc Aldrich.

At this, red flame spurted up before Doc's eyes. A sledge-hammer was clapped against the base of his spine, a strong stick was whanged against the back of his knees, and the whole earth rose to strike him in the face with violence.

He slept.

When he awakened, a wet handkerchief lay across his eyes.

"Poor kid!" said Doc Aldrich.

"Which kid is that?" asked the voice of him that should have been dead.

Doc Aldrich sat bolt erect. "You ain't a ghost?" he demanded. "Oh, holy smoke, how everything is spinning around in front of me. Where do you carry that sandbag? Up your sleeve?"

"Here," said Archibald, and closed his right hand.

As a great artist of the squared circle has said: "It's all in the way you hold your hand. You bust your bones, or you bust the other fellow's bones. It's all in the way you hold your hand."

The way that Archibald held it was the right way. Doc Aldrich, who had once been a featherweight and had aspired to walk to fame along the rosined pathway, saw and at once understood.

"I seem to remember," said Doc. "It was a straight right with a little poison on the end of it . . . a little hook, I mean."

"It was a right cross," said Archibald. "And it happened to hit the button."

"Not a button, but a buzzer," said Doc Aldrich, "and you still got your foot on it. Look here, kid, where did you learn all that nasty stuff about crosses that was never found in any church? Might I be permitted?"

"You might," said Archibald, and proffered his left arm.

Upon the apparent fat of that arm the fingers of Doc Aldrich closed.

"All right . . . ready," he said.

The fingers of Doc began to bulge outward. A quiver ran through the sleeve. Suddenly, it appeared to be filled.

"Holy smoke!" murmured Doc Aldrich. "And yet you look . . . oh, well, it ain't so bad. I thought that it was some boob that had sandbagged me, but I see that it's one of the Irvings . . . the last of that name."

"I thank you very much," said Archibald.

"All I would like to know," said Doc, "is how long does a noose need to strangle you, or would the boys give me a long enough drop to break my neck. I hate the long wait. I'd like a running start when I'm on my way." He added thoughtfully: "How much reward have they put up for me?"

"None that I've heard of," said Archibald.

The little man sprang to his feet in a fury, although he was still so dizzy that he staggered and kept his balance with only the greatest difficulty.

"No reward on me?" he shouted. "No reward! Ain't a good man-sized gunfight and a hoss stealing . . . ain't that worth a reward in this man's country, now I ask you?"

"It seems hard," said Archibald, "not to recognize talent like that."

"They'll bump me off like a rat," said Doc Aldrich. "There won't even be no newspaper clipping. Ma's heart will be broke, and no mistake."

"Look here," said Archibald, "what makes you so gloomy? Is it time for me to take you to the caboose?"

"No," said Doc Aldrich sourly. "After me trying to blow your mid-section loose from your ribs, it's time you kissed me good bye and told me to beat it. It's time for you to do the fairy godmother."

"Close up that talk," said Mr. Archibald Irving politely, "because you rattle, Doc. I needed some of the things in that wallet. And so I had to tag you. Which I admit was a dirty trick. But as soon as that bump wears off your jaw, I hope that you'll forget about it."

A dark flush covered the face of Doc Aldrich. Then, in silence, he began to roll a cigarette. He lighted it and smoked slowly, growing still redder and redder.

"It seems to me," he said finally, in a husky voice, "it seems to me, as how I've made a skunk out of myself."

"Tush!" said Archibald. "Hand me the makings, will you? By the way, here's your gun."

And from the ground he raised the Colt, and, holding it by the long, gleaming barrel, he placed the handle in the grip of the little man.

Mr. Aldrich took the Colt with due reverence, and then shoved it slowly into the holster. He took off his hat and scratched his head, filled with thought. He said at last: "Mister Irving, I suppose that I'm about the first man in the county really to meet you. I would sort of like to shake hands in honor of the day."

"Tickled to death!" said Archibald.

Chapter Thirteen

"A PARTNER"

After a little time Archibald said: "There stands only one charge against you, Doc."

"Hoss stealing. That's all. Ain't that enough? Outside of shooting down a man. . . ."

"The man you shot down won't press any charge against you."

"Good old Jerry. No, he'll only wait till he gets well, and then, as soon as he's in practice with his gun, he'll come to blow me in two."

"As for the horse stealing," offered Irving, "I think that a hundred dollars would settle that for you."

"And where am I to get the hundred? Take it from Ma, and her about to sell out to Fraser?"

"We'll send word to her to hold on and not to sell. Any forced quick sale to that pirate is sure to be a heavy loss. And as for the hundred, I'll find it for you."

Doc Aldrich inhaled a long breath. "This ain't a fairy tale," he said. "Also, I am awake. Go right on talking, Mister Irving. I'm having a wonderful day dream. You give me a hundred, which squares me with Thomas for swiping his horse. And then. . . ."

"And then," said Mr. Irving, "I buy some groceries, *et cetera,* today, and I move them into the old house by the lake. And you come in there to live with me."

"Say," said Doc Aldrich, "would you mind telling me

what you take that makes you this way? But what's my job to
be in that house?"

"Keeping my neck from being broken."

"Do I smile when you say that?"

"You do not, I hope. The fact is, Doc, that I've started
playing a game with a pair of tigers, and, if one of them tags
me, it will be with a paw that will tear me right in two. Do you
understand? There are two men in this county who will very
shortly want my scalp. One of them wants it already."

"Then why not hang out at the hotel, where you'll have a
crowd around you to watch what might happen?"

"A Western crowd," said Archibald, "makes a pretty good
audience for a shooting, but it isn't apt to take a hand. Not
until the bullets begin to come its way. No, I prefer to be off
by myself, and not have to keep my eye on every face in that
same crowd we were speaking of. I'll stay out in the house by
the lake and you'll mail to Thomas a hundred dollars which
I'll give you. Then we'll both keep our eyes open . . . because
we're going to need vigilance, I can tell you."

"Captain," said little Doc Aldrich, "you give the orders,
and I'll try to keep step."

The buckboard and team that Archibald Irving hired in
Irvington was loaded heavily. Then he drove slowly out the
dusty way to the valley, and down to the edge of the lake.
Here, safe from all observation, he and the waiting Doc carried the provisions into the kitchen. Presently, the fire was
burning in the stove, and Doc Aldrich was preparing to eat
his first real meal in some time. His hundred dollars and a
letter to his mother had been entrusted to the mail. There was
nothing remaining except to wait.

When the sunset came, Mr. Aldrich said: "Only I don't see
why you should sit here where they'll expect to find you."

"What do you suggest, Doc?"

"Why, I suggest the last place where they'll be expecting you. Come in the back yard of the man that wants to get you the most. He'll never expect you there in calling distance of him, will he? Go right up and sit down under Watson's window."

"Watson?" cried Archibald. "Who under heaven has mentioned his name?"

Doc merely grunted. "It's all right," he said. "I'm blind. I ain't seen nothing. Or if I did, I suppose that he *gave* you that check all endorsed so pretty . . . for ten thousand iron men."

Archibald was forced to light another cigarette.

"It gives me a queer tickle in the innards, Doc," he said, "for you to read my mind like this. In the meantime, it is getting dark enough for a pretty respectable murder. And I think there's something in what you suggest. Let's leave this house, and leave it now."

"The more *pronto* the better."

They left the house and took a boat that was moored at the edge of the water. This boat they rowed in leisurely fashion, like men about to do a little fishing along the surface of the lake. Opposite the next point, they paused, as though this place suited them. A moment later they were rowing on again.

Among the trees near the house, a solitary watcher had observed all these motions of the shadowy pair. As soon as he had satisfied himself that they were merely fishing and not apt to return for some time, he curled himself up under a tree and proceeded to the enjoyment of a quiet pipe.

In the thickening dusk at the farther end of the lake, the prow of the borrowed boat grated sharply among the pebbles of the beach. A moment later, the two rowers were away up the valley side through a winding trail, with Doc Aldrich steadily cursing all traveling by foot.

When he paused to pant and rest, he asked: "About that damned automatic. You always carry it filled up with blanks?"

"I always do," said Archibald.

"Now look here, Irving. You're a fine feller, and all that, and as clean as a whip, and most probable you're smart, for your own section of the country. But that sort of thing ain't apt to get you along very far around here. It really ain't! If you pull a gun in the West, you want to know beforehand that you *have* to pull it. And when you have to pull it, shoot to kill . . . shoot mighty straight, and you be particular about the killing. Blank cartridges ain't never used out here except on the stage."

"I'll tell you," answered Archibald Irving. "If I pulled out a real Forty-Five, I could not hit the side of a barn with it. And I would not really load an automatic any more than I would load a garden hose with poison . . . because I would be too liable to spatter lead all over the bystanders."

"But why carry it at all?" asked Doc, nodding his agreement with these last two remarks.

"Because," said Archibald, "at close quarters . . . like a poker game, a little gun like that talks twice as loud as a big one . . . because it always comes from an unexpected place. And it isn't often, really, that a man has to shoot . . . if he has the nerve to hold his gun steady and look the other fellow in the eye."

Doc Aldrich started to answer with some heat, but he presently changed his mind and shook his head. "All right," he stated. "Every man's way is the best for him."

In the meantime, they had climbed up the valley side, and they were fast approaching the cloud of trees that grew upon the new estate of Mr. William Watson. They did not turn in at the great wrought-iron gates. Instead, they climbed the huge wall, and so found themselves within the park.

"Here," said Archibald, "we're trespassers, and the owner of the place has a perfect right to use guns on us. Moreover, Doc, in case you have any doubts about the matter, I want to tell you that in case Watson should see me here, or have a hint that I am on his ground, he would move heaven and earth to get me, and salt me away with lead. And he would not stop with me. He would be perfectly glad to remove any others who happened to be at my side. D'you understand?"

"Like I had read it in a book," said Doc Aldrich, grinning.

"And where'll we go now?" asked Archibald.

"Up as close to the fire as we can get," said Doc. "Right up toward the house, but watching our step pretty careful, if it's just the same to you."

And that was exactly the manner of their procedure. Stealing from tree to tree and from shrub to shrub, they drew nearer and nearer to the flaring windows of the big house. It was still not quite the utter black of the night. Out of the western sky enough light was reflected to outline everything in distinct hoods of black. The shining of the stars was still small and uncertain.

By that same shimmering light, the active eye of Doc Aldrich now made out something that lived and moved before them. He gripped the arm of his companion, and pointed. What they saw was, indeed, worthy of their wonder, for the man ahead of them was moving exactly as they moved.

"It means mischief," whispered Archibald. "And unless I'm badly mistaken, Watson should be glad that he has me for an enemy. I think that we may be the savers of his scalp to-night."

"What'll we do?" whispered Doc. "Move out of these crowded quarters?"

"We'll have a better look at our friend, yonder."

And to the amusement of Doc, Archibald began to slip forward.

"With no bullet in your gun . . . ?" gasped out Doc.

Archibald struck away his restraining hand and wormed his way ahead. He was no trained hunter, but instinct has planted in the heart of every man enough skill in this game of life and death called trailing. He stalked the shadowy form of the stranger in sufficient speed and silence, until he came up behind the very bush that sheltered the other from the light of the window of the big house, just ahead. Here, most opportunely, the other turned his head.

At once, Archibald Irving was aware of the blunt nose and the whole brutal profile of Charlie, the watchdog of Mr. Fraser.

His presence there was self-explanatory. This was to be Fraser's way of getting revenge for the blows that he had received that same morning.

Archibald straightened to his knees.

"Charlie," he called softly, and stretched forth the automatic. "Charlie . . . up with your hands."

Charlie turned, or, rather, he whirled with his fist prepared.

Oh, well for Archibald had he taken the advice of Doc Aldrich, given so heartily on this same day. But there was no bullet in this automatic to arrest the lunge of the brute before him. And something told him that it would be useless to fire a blank at this charging creature. He raised the gun to use it as a club, but a ponderous fist dashed into his face as he did so, and flattened him against the earth.

Chapter Fourteen

"CHARLIE COMES ACROSS"

There was no possibility of resistance. That blow was dashed home with far too much accuracy. It flattened Archibald and shocked every whit of consciousness out of his brain. Charlie dropped his knees on the chest of his helpless enemy and clapped the muzzle of his revolver against the temple.

A half of a second and Archibald should have been winging his way toward heaven. But Charlie recollected that this was not the only duty on which he had started forth, upon this occasion. He altered his mind, and, gripping the gun by the barrel, he prepared to batter out the brains of Archibald Irving.

He swung the gun up once, to freshen his grip and give himself a surer aim, just as the golf player waggles the club before striking home. As Charlie raised the gun the second and final time, he received a clip from the steel barrel of a Colt leveled along his own skull and sent home with terrible force.

Charlie dropped flat and limp upon his victim.

When Charlie recovered himself a little, he heard a faintly groaning voice saying: "God bless you, Doc. But I wish that you had got here a second quicker. I think the brute has bashed all of my ribs with his knees. What a filthy beast it is, Doc. But I hope that you didn't smash his skull."

"I didn't," said Doc. "It was like banging a chunk of stone. That head of his must be reënforced with ribs of steel." Then

91

he said to Charlie: "Steady, sonny. Don't try to move about too lively. This little baby has got six chunks of lead all labeled . . . 'Home, Charlie.' So watch yourself, lad. You can sit up. But don't fumble for either of those hidden guns. Because I have them both."

Charlie made no answer. He sat up and hung his head in a sullen silence. When they ordered him to rise, he raised his voice and made most startling answer: "Look here," he said, "I can see by the way you talk that you ain't been invited in here any more than I was. Now, you two leave me be and beat it, or I'll raise a yapping that'll bring every man in that house out here with shotguns. And that's what old Watson trusts to . . . shotguns!"

Archibald felt a tremor of uncertainty run through him. And certainly he would not have known how to answer this sudden and unexpected challenge. But Doc Aldrich had no such doubts. Before the wide mouth of Charlie had finished this speech the steel muzzle of a Colt was jammed between his lips, splintering one of the front teeth.

"Why, you fool," said Doc, "do you think that we're amateurs, maybe? You murdering swine, you're Charlie Bostwick, ain't you? Yes, sir. Well, Charlie, I'm Doc Aldrich. You disremember the day that you handed my ma some of your lip at Fraser's office. But I ain't forgot. So watch yourself, old son, and stand up and come along with us, nice and polite. Because it wouldn't hurt my feelings *none* to have to blow your head off, old-timer. Do you hear me talk?"

It was apparent that Charlie *did* hear. He arose most meekly and walked slowly ahead and away from the house of Watson.

"Where shall we take him," asked Doc in a whisper, "and what shall we do with him?"

He was surprised to find that Archibald had lost all of his

calm surety. He was fairly trembling with excitement.

"We'll take him to that little deserted shack halfway down the hill," said Archibald. "And fast, Doc . . . fast. I think that I know why Charlie was up there. If I can get a written statement out of him . . . oh, man, I hardly had dared to hope for anything like this. God bless you for sending us up here to the house of Watson."

"I dunno that I follow your drift," admitted Doc. "But I fail to see what you'll get out of this Charlie."

"Let me do the thinking for both of us, for a while," said Archibald. "There's the shack. You can see the angle of the roof of it just beyond the wall of the Watson place."

It lay, in fact, hardly more than a furlong along the valley from the edge of the Watson place—too close, perhaps, considering all the dangers that were surrounding Archibald and his companion at this moment. Young Irving could not wait.

Into that ruined little shell of a house he led Charlie. With a handful of dry, dead splinters, he kindled a tiny fire, and by the light of that he surveyed the stolid face of Charlie.

"Now, Charlie," he began, "I'm going to ask you to write down a little confession for me. And when you've written it down, I'll turn you loose. I'm going to ask you why you went up to Watson's house?"

Charlie replied calmly: "Me girl is doing the cooking there. I was goin' up to see her, you know."

Doc Aldrich laughed aloud.

Archibald answered: "Do you usually wear three guns when you go to call on your girl?"

"I wear three guns day in and day out," said Charlie. "I need 'em, and I wear 'em. And that's all there is to that."

"That's all there is to that," mocked Doc Aldrich gloomily. "But I'm wishing, now, that I had the half of the names of the men that you've had the butchering of, you black swine."

The broad upper lip of Charlie curled in sullen scorn, and he shrugged his shoulders. "You'll never have the knowing of that," he said, "unless I tell it to you, sometime when I've got my fist fixed in your windpipe, chokin' off the air slow and gradual."

He was not a pleasant man, this Charlie. He had the look and the voice and the snarl of a brute, and his little pig eyes burned and glittered at the two strangers.

Archibald Irving persevered: "All that I want with you is a little scribbling on a sheet of paper, Charlie."

"I can't write," said Charlie.

"You lie," said Archibald calmly.

"Do I lie?" answered Charlie with a gust of fury. "You can beat me or shoot me or throw me to the dogs, but I'll talk to you no more, and I'll pleasure you in nothing. And that's the end of that."

Archibald Irving stood back and whistled. "Dear, dear," he said, "what a violent man. I think that we had better begin with tying him, Doc."

"Aye, and we should have done that before if. . . ."

Charlie had seemed curled in composure against the wall of the building, with the light from the little fire playing with a flicker of shadow across his face, but now he leaped into action and headed with a bound for the door. Doc Aldrich had his back turned at that moment, in the act of dragging a length of cord from his pocket. When he whirled, there was nothing but time for a snap shot—and Archibald Irving in line for the bullet as well as Charlie.

No doubt Charlie had counted upon this fact. He made only one mistake, which was in taking Archibald Irving a trifle too lightly, a mistake in which he could have been forgiven, having mastered him once so easily. He picked his time for his rush when there was nothing between him and his freedom saving the plump form of Archie. Then he charged like a maddened bull, prepared to smash his way to freedom with a single stroke of his massive fist.

He was not at all prepared for what followed—which was the delivery of a straight right of the neatest and cleanest variety. It lodged not on the chin but on the side of his face, so that Charlie was not stunned. However, his charge was checked, and he was put back upon his heels, and, before he could right himself, two more blows followed—two blows that Doc Aldrich thought he recognized, because they were delivered with a rise and fall of the puncher's body. And the fists, snapping across the shoulders of Charlie, landed squarely home.

Still he did not drop to the floor, but he staggered drunkenly back until his shoulders struck the opposite wall of the house. And before he could right himself again, Doc Aldrich had secured the hands of the warrior with a stout twine. And then another length of twine was passed around his ankles. He lay secure and easy. Sitting, now, with his shoulders against the wall, he glared with unabated ferocity at his captors and regardless of the blood that flowed down his face. Doc Aldrich, at the direction of his companion, swabbed the blood away.

And he made free comment as he worked: "Here's where the first one landed. Oh, a pretty neat one. If you had diagrammed that punch and laid it out with a surveyor's line, you couldn't have hit a straighter punch! It just split the skin over his cheek bone. And here's where the left cross got in. It must have busted a tooth inside his face and cut the cheek against it. And here's where the other . . . the right cross, got in . . . oh, Charlie, did you know what hit you, that time? Ain't it a beauty, that punch? And where does he pack them beauties? You should feel his arm, boy, and then you'll understand, just the way your brother Doc understands."

Archibald Irving said: "It looks to me as though you have him cleaned up enough now. I didn't want to have him in such shape that any of his attention would be taken away from what we're going to do to him. I wanted him to have all his wits free to concentrate on this. Just help me off with his shoes, Doc, will you?"

Doc, bewildered, obeyed. Shoes and socks were tugged from the feet of the prisoner.

"Now," said Archibald Irving, "we don't want to try any of the things that Charlie mentioned as not caring about. We want to try something which is entirely new. And I don't think that our friend has mentioned fire, do you? Draw him up to the blaze, Doc, and toast his toes for him until he finds his voice."

He seasoned this remark with a broad wink at Doc; the latter responded with a flash of joyous understanding in his eye. He freshened the little blaze, and then the naked feet of Charlie were dragged closer and closer to the fire.

"Take it easy, Doc," said Archibald Irving. "He might as well have it slowly. Then he'll appreciate the full beauty of being as warm as possible."

Here he actually brought the horny bottoms of the feet of Charlie in touch with the flame. There was a gasp and a snort, and Charlie's feet were violently jerked back.

"Tie him bodily to that board," directed Archibald calmly. "We can't be bothered with his twistings and turnings. We'll have some talk out of this lad, or else we'll leave only a cinder of him behind us. I'd as soon burn him as a slice of bacon!"

"I b'lieve you!" gasped out Charlie. "You *would* torture

me . . . and you one of them fine Irvings!"

"I'm a degenerate son, not worthy of those brave and bold men," said Archibald Irving blandly. "But every man must live in his own way, Charlie, as perhaps you yourself know. Don't be too hard upon me, Charlie. But tell me that you will write out the truth of why you went to the house of Watson. And in the first place, tell us what that truth is."

"Never," said Charlie.

"Doc, we'll give him to the fire all right this time. The pig needs singeing before he'll believe that I mean what I say. Besides, I'd be rather glad to give him sore feet. . . ."

"Hold up," snarled Charlie. "I never seen such a devil in all my born days. I'll tell you what you want to know. I come up there not really to see the cook, though I know her. But me and the gardener . . . I used to know him in Fulsom. Him and me done a stretch there together, once. And I thought that maybe all of the heavy silver in the Watson house might be sneaked out, some night. . . ."

"A very broad lie, Charlie," said Archibald Irving. "You would never have gone stealing through the grounds to talk to him. You would have made a convenient meeting place. Now, tell me the truth!" He added: "And this is the last chance I give you. You talk out the truth this time and then write it down, or I'll burn you so that you'll never walk again . . . before I give you another *chance* to talk."

The sweat rolled out upon the forehead of Charlie.

"Nothing that I say can please you none," he muttered.

"You're wrong, Charlie. The truth will please me a very good deal. So let me have it, and at once. I can't waste any more time."

Charlie was silent—it was plain that he was in the greatest distress. He said at length: "Mister Irving, it was the old man that persuaded me to it. I don't mind fists. And I've used the sandbag, here and there. But I hate guns. . . ."

"So much that you carry three of them. But continue, Charlie. This is not a promising start."

"It was that old rat, Fraser. He got me to do it. Partly by begging me, and partly by giving me . . . offering me, I mean. . . ."

"Search his pockets," snapped Archibald.

And the willing Doc extracted from the pockets of the writhing victim a thick wad of bills.

"Fifteen hundred in hard cash," said Doc presently.

"Was Watson's life worth that much to Fraser?" asked Archibald.

"How did you know?"

"That confession," said Archibald, "is enough to hang you, my friend. There are two of us to swear to it. And by far the best thing that you can do is to sit down at once and prove yourself a literary artist . . . I have a bit of paper here, and a pen. You can write small on it, Charlie."

Charlie, without a word, allowed his head to sink.

"Free his hands," said Archibald, and the thing was done. "Right here, by the light of this little fire, Charlie."

And so there it was that Charlie wrote out his confession, pushing the pen with a reluctant shudder across the surface of the paper, writing small but clearly enough. And at last he ended and signed his name—his true name—a name which was strange in that county that had known Charlie so long.

"Now we are going to leave you tied here, and we are going down to see Mister Fraser. What is your signal with him, Charlie?"

Chapter Fifteen

"THE COUP"

It was a long time since Mr. Fraser had slept. Now he had fallen into a doze over his labors in the office that night. All the night before, he had not closed his eyes, beyond a moment here and there. This night a burning anxiety had kept him awake in spite of his weariness. However, fatigue will have its way. And at last Mr. Fraser's head bowed low, and lower.

He was on the verge of complete slumber, when he started to his feet with his heart thundering. There had been a heavy knock on the street door—a heavy knock that was now repeated twice, a long interval between each stroke.

Mr. Fraser's eyes gleamed. If you have seen the glittering eye of the ferret when it rushes in upon the nest of birds, you have an idea of the picture that Mr. Fraser made as he hurried down the passage. At the outer door he paused. "Is it you, Charlie?" he asked eagerly.

For answer, there was an inarticulate snarl that made Mr. Fraser shudder with pleasure. Such was the voice of a man who had succeeded in the business that was in hand for this evening.

He unlocked the door, but first of all he opened it only a crack to make sure. But just as he released the door a trifle, two heavy shoulders were thrust against it. The edge of the door leaped out of the hands of old Mr. Fraser, and he found before him the proscribed Aldrich, and Mr. Archibald Irving—that simple youth.

"I've brought a little message to you from Charlie," Archibald stated.

"Close the door," said Mr. Fraser, wringing his hands. "All is lost. I see in your face that all is lost. Close the door. Gentlemen, gentlemen, did the dog talk? But come in quickly . . . you'll find that I can listen . . . to reason . . . to a great deal of reason!"

You observe that the mind of Mr. Fraser moved a little more quickly than that of Mr. Watson. Mr. Watson had to have defeat explained to him with a chart, but Mr. Fraser recognized it while it was still upon the wing.

They all sat together in the office.

"We will let Charlie speak for us first," said Archibald. "I'll read this aloud, Doc, if you'll keep your eye fixed on this slippery old devil. I beg your pardon, Mister Fraser, but the truth will out, you know."

As Mr. Fraser made no answer, but sat with his chin fallen upon his chest, a deplorably sunken figure, Archibald read deliberately and slowly:

This evening, right after supper, when I come on for night duty, Mr. Alexander Fraser, of Irvington, that I work for, called me into his office and said that he had a job for me that was worth a lot of money and wanted to know if I could use five hundred. . . .

"It's enough!" said Fraser, groaning. "That is enough. I. . . ."

"And now," Archibald said. "Mister Watson is dead. For fifteen hundred dollars. However, when you hang, Mister Fraser, you will pay the right price . . . all of it."

"Gentlemen . . . gentlemen," Mr. Fraser began. "You will be reasonable, I know."

"Reasonable, if you wish reason. For Mister Aldrich, here, we'll have to have the mortgage on his mother's ranch, and a little capital to run on. . . ."

"It shall be done," said Mr. Fraser with a groan. "It shall be done."

"My own price is much smaller."

A light of joy appeared in the eye of Mr. Fraser.

"My own price," said Archibald, "is only the return of properties that already belong to me, by right. You committed a legal theft. Now I grant you permission to undo that wrong. And you will make over to me by your deed all of your properties in Irving Valley."

"What?" screamed Fraser, "a million . . . !"

"Is it worth as much as that?" Archibald asked, grinning. "But still, I'll have to have it. If you have made certain improvements in the meantime, I am very sorry to take those along with the land.

"Man, man, I said I would listen to reason, but. . . ."

"You fool," Archibald said sternly, "do you think that the murdered man on the hill . . . ?"

And Mr. Fraser collapsed.

For a whole hour he was busy in his office, writing out and signing certain documents for the benefit of Archibald Irving. When he was ended, the two men stood up for their departure, leaving the banker sitting with fallen head beside his desk, and his hands pressed against his face. More bitterly than half his blood he begrudged the acts of justice that he had that night performed.

"And, by the way," said Archibald from the doorway, "I ought to tell you, lest you have an unnecessary weight on your conscience, that our friend Watson was not murdered, after all. It was only the good intention that Charlie confessed, if you had had the patience to hear the confession through. Good night, Mister Fraser."

But Mr. Fraser did not lift his head. He was a thoroughly beaten man.

The rehabilitation of Doc Aldrich was a matter that was never thoroughly understood, because Archibald Irving's part in it was wisely concealed from the public gaze. It was known, of course, that Thomas had withdrawn his charge, and that he had been paid in full the value of the stolen horse. It was further known that Jerry Swinton was unwilling to pursue any legal action against his conqueror.

The greatest mystery, however, was the transfer of the lands of Irving Valley back to Archibald Irving. To this mystery not even the lawyer, John Vincent, became an initiate.

Two afternoons after the interview between Mr. Fraser and the two who carried Charlie's confession, a pair of interviews occurred all in the same hour.

One took place on the hillside above Irving Valley, where Mr. Fraser and Mr. Watson met by accident. And Watson took the first step.

"Sandy," he said, "if I tell you that I'm sorry for what happened between us . . . and if I tell you that I got as bad a licking as you did, will you forgive me?"

"Billy," said Mr. Fraser, "I've had it dinned in upon me that I've become an old man, but I would give up a million dollars to know how *you* lost your share of the valley?"

"It begins," said Mr. Watson, "with a plump-looking young man. . . ."

"Young Irving, of course."

"Aye, that very man."

"Watson, we used a silent partnership before. But from now on I think that we'd better take advantage of an open one. We'll *need* it, if that young devil begins to operate in the same county with us, unless we're to have our shoulders driven against the wall."

Mr. Watson nodded gravely.

"It's true," he agreed. "He has the real touch of financial genius . . . and youth on his side against us, to say nothing of a grudge that is as sharp as a razor blade."

At the very time that this conversation was taking place on one side of Irving Valley, Mr. Archibald Irving had stepped into the office of Vincent, the lawyer.

"And how," said Vincent coldly, "has the time been running on with you. Fox hunting?"

"A rotten country for running foxes," said Archibald. "I've just been all over the valley. As a matter of fact, I've decided to go on with my uncle's schemes there. All of them, Vincent. Even to the building of the last fence. Foxes be damned. There is too much money in that ground."

"Ah," said Mr. Vincent, for as yet not a whisper of what had happened had gone abroad upon the air of Irvington. "Ah, Archie, you are contemplating buying out the two owners, then?"

His dryness did not seem to affect the youth.

"As a matter of fact, I have agreed with them on that point," he said. "I have bought them out already." And he placed the deeds upon the desk.

Mr. Vincent looked through them as fast as he could, for his head was swimming and a black mist was whirling before his eyes. He said at length: "Merciful heaven, Archie. I never dreamed that you had really inherited any fortune other than this of your uncle."

"I haven't," said Archibald.

"But it says here . . . for value received . . . on both

deeds . . . and . . . what under heaven can it all mean?"

"Why," said Archibald, "as you know, if you've ridden after a fox, it isn't always the fastest horse that is in at the kill. And it isn't always money that has the highest value. However, I think they are both satisfied with their half of the bargain, and I'm sure that I am satisfied with mine."

The Outlaw Redeemer

Chapter One

"THE WILD GOOSE"

These are the generations of Hubert Dunleven.

In the beginning, out of a mist of Scottish and Irish, there appeared Robert Dunleven who had reason to flee from his home country to the young United States. He took to wife Little Beaver, a full-blooded Iroquois maiden, and they begat Edward. And Edward had reason to flee from his native state to Canada, where he took to wife Estelle, the daughter of a French-Canadian, and they begat Pierre. And Pierre had reason to flee from the country to the island of Jamaica, far south, where he took to wife Anne, the daughter of an English planter. And they begat Lawrence who had reason to flee from his native island to Texas where he took to wife Carmelita, the daughter of a Spanish idler, and they begat Hubert, who had reason to flee all the days of his young life, and who got himself names, to wit: Shorty, alias Bunch, alias The Duke. And these are the generations of Hubert Dunleven.

Now these are the generations of John Tipton.

In the beginning from stalwart and honest people of Devon there appeared John Tipton, who became a constable in the service of his king and country, and he was a mighty man. He took to wife Rose, the daughter of a Devon farmer near Barnstaple, and they begat John, who was a mighty man and served his king and country as a constable. He took to wife Margaret, the daughter of a Devon farmer near

Barnstaple, and they begat John, who was a mighty man and served his king and country as a constable. He took to wife Elizabeth, the daughter of a Devon farmer near Barnstaple, and they begat John, who was a mighty man, and served his king and country as a constable. He took to wife Diana, the daughter of a Devon farmer near Barnstaple, and they begat John, who was a mighty man, and served his king and country as a constable. And he took to wife Kate, the daughter of a Devon farmer near Barnstaple, and they begat John Tipton, who felt a call for the blue sea and traveled across the Atlantic, and reached a new country, and went to Texas, and became a ranger in the service of the state. These are the generations of John Tipton, who was a mighty man.

When this John Tipton was a mere youth with the rose of Devon still in his cheeks and the love of his new country bright in his eyes, he rubbed elbows, in a crowd at a rodeo, with another no older than himself, a short fellow with a stern, ugly face, with wide shoulders and long-dangling arms. And the short man turned and smote the boy from Devon upon the root of the nose so that the blood burst forth. Then John Tipton, of Barnstaple and San Antone, poised his long arms and struck Hubert Dunleven to the dust, out of which Hubert rose again. They fought long, and great was the combat between them until Hubert Dunleven fixèd his hands on the throat of John Tipton, and men with the barrels of revolvers beat him over the head to make him loose his hold.

However, John Tipton came within eyeshot of death, and, when he was recovered, he took thought and offered himself for service with the rangers. There he studied hard how to shoot swift and straight, and how to ride wild horses, and how to travel far and sleep light, and how to read the trail and hold his tongue and tell the truth, but not too much of it. And most of all, he labored day by day at two twin arts—how to box and how to wrestle. For a memory and a horror were never out of his mind of a day when a short man with wide shoulders and long arms had met with him and brought him to the verge of death with a grip of steel.

Then on a day there were tidings of a gambling hall and a shooting fracas, and the captain of the rangers sent the blue-eyed man of Devon riding to capture the slayer.

Between the root of a cliff and a winding yellow river frothed with white, John Tipton came on a wide-shouldered man with a dark, stern, ugly face—came suddenly on him, so that there was no time for drawing of weapons. They grappled on horseback. They fell writhing beneath the hoofs of the horses. And there a blow from the hoof of his own mount stretched the fugitive senseless.

And John Tipton of Barnstaple and San Antone, in the service of his conscience and his country, rode serenely into the ranger camp with Hubert Dunleven in irons on a led horse.

That very night, Dunleven slipped his manacles, gagged and bound his guard, and rode off on a stolen horse. The horse of John Tipton himself.

Then John Tipton rode slowly and patiently on that northern and western trail. He followed it north, and he followed it west. Many another duty and many another quest fell in between, but two years later, in an empty boxcar of a train that was crawling across the Continental Divide, Tipton found a wide-shouldered man with a dark, stern, and ugly face.

Their guns they tore from the hands of one another. They fought with the weapons that God had given them until Tipton fell into a swoon, and he wakened to find the criminal gone and a brakeman leaning above him.

So John Tipton waited until his wounds were healed.

Then he labored patiently and steadily in drawing a revolver and striking the distant target with his rifle, and most of all in boxing and wrestling.

After that he took the trail again. More deeds were attributed to Hubert Dunleven, and he had gained the first two of his names, Shorty and Bunch, both of which were derived from his physical peculiarities. Many crimes were laid up against him in the mind of the law, that forgets not, and above all in the mind of the servant of the law, John Tipton.

There were more fights over cards, fights over liquor, and wild rumors of crusades of rascality that Hubert Dunleven carried south of the Río Grande, where the skins of men were as swarthy as his own, and their eyes and hair as black. There were dead men upon those southern trails of Dunleven, but only ghostly rumors came back to the northland and to the ear of John Tipton.

But at last the trail crossed the Río Grande again, and Tipton, like a strong eagle, struck away for the sight of Hubert Dunleven. Still another long year followed. The trail was often lost, and often it was caught again, and followed by foot, by horse, by boat, by train, until at last on a raft that sagged slowly down the current of the Mississippi, the two men met and fought again, fist to fist, and grip to grip, until a long-drive right crashed fairly home upon the jaw of Hubert Dunleven and dropped him upon his back, to rise no more for the battle.

Again John Tipton brought his captive into the hands of the law, and this time he reached the jail and stood his trial. Murder the district attorney pitched upon, very awkwardly. There were plenty of other strings to the bow. There were twenty other proved crimes that might have been used to keep Dunleven behind the bars for half a dozen lifetimes. But when it came to murder—well, it was proved in the courtroom that Hubert Dunleven had formed the invariable habit of standing to his enemies and meeting them face to face. If they used bare hands, he used bare hands, also. If they caught up a cudgel, he selected another. If they would try the edge of the cruel knife, he was one with them, and if they reached for guns—they died.

Manslaughter, or some such vague matter, it might be called. But murder? Not in the State of Texas, not in that Year of our Lord.

That was the district attorney's mistake, and he saw twelve good men and true of the state stand up and declare the prisoner not guilty. It threw the district attorney into such a passion that he forgot to have Hubert Dunleven arrested on another charge before he left the courtroom, and, therefore, the wild goose took wing again.

Another year or more, then, before John Tipton was on the trail. And for eighteen months he followed it. Much, much had happened in the two and a half years before he met Dunleven again. Dunleven had risen to a higher station in the world of crime. Somewhere south of the Río Grande he had met a lady, men said. But whether or not it was all feminine influence, no one could tell. Only it was known that, when he reappeared in the northland, his appearance and his manners had undergone a change.

Somewhere in the south he acquired a sudden polish. Book knowledge he had always had, or enough of it to do him. But now he was no longer the abysmal brute. He dressed almost fastidiously. He had learned everything except how to smile. Even his crimes took on a different nature. He appeared as a prowler in Manhattan. Sundry rich gulls subscribed to his schemes, and he slipped away from New York with a heavier wallet, and his third and last nickname—The Duke.

On the trail of The Duke rode John Tipton, his cheeks still bright with Devon roses, and miles by thousands lay behind him before he encountered the arch-enemy head to head as their two horses turned a narrow angle on a bridle path. They flung themselves at one another in silent fury.

The fists of John Tipton never drove harder or faster, and his arms and shoulders were never so heavy. But he could not beat down that shifting, springing form. His power ebbed; a bone-crushing blow on the side of the head made his knees sag. He tried to fall into a clinch, but a lifting uppercut dumped him into a thousand leagues of darkness.

When he recovered his fists, he found that his feet and his hands were free. But his guns, his wallet, his papers were all in the possession of the wide-shouldered, stern-faced man who sat above him on horseback and looked calmly down upon him.

"Now," said Hubert Dunleven, "take a good look at me, Tipton, because, if you have good sense, this is the last time that you'll ever lay eyes on me. Remember that, John. I'm tired of being dogged by you. And if you have any doubt about me being the better man, stand up and we'll fight it out again!"

Join the Western Book Club
and GET 4 FREE* BOOKS NOW!
A $19.96 VALUE!

Yes! I want to subscribe to the Western Book Club.

Please send me my **4 FREE* BOOKS**. I have enclosed $2.00 for shipping/handling. Each month I'll receive the four newest Leisure Western selections to preview for 10 days. If I decide to keep them, I will pay the Special Members Only discounted price of just $3.36 each, a total of $13.44, plus $2.00 shipping/handling ($19.50 US in Canada). This is a **SAVINGS OF AT LEAST $6.00** off the bookstore price. There is no minimum number of books I must buy, and I may cancel the program at any time. In any case, the **4 FREE* BOOKS** are mine to keep.

*In Canada, add $5.00 shipping/handling per order
for the first shipment. For all future shipments to
Canada, the cost of membership is $16.25 US,
which includes shipping and handling.
(All payments must be made in US dollars.)

NAME: _____

ADDRESS: _____

CITY: _____ STATE: _____

COUNTRY: _____ ZIP: _____

TELEPHONE: _____

E-MAIL: _____

SIGNATURE: _____

Chapter Two

"A MISTAKE"

Now, of all the honest fighting stock in the world, there is none better than the British bulldog. And among the British there is no truer battler than your Devon man. He fights partly because he loves fighting. And he fights usually to the death, because he dreads death less than the shame of defeat.

So John Tipton, sitting up half groggy from the effects of the terrible blow that had floored him, had the light of battle glinting back in his eyes at once. He felt, in his heart of hearts, that for all his skill, and for all his superior poundage, he had neither craft nor power to meet the sinewy might of those long arms and those wide shoulders. If he were a bulldog, yonder was a terrier, just as pugnacious, just as aggressive, just as valiant to the bitter end, and, in addition, cruelly fast of hand and feet.

Yet, notwithstanding that he felt he could not match this fellow, it never as much as occurred to John Tipton that he should give up the fight. But as he set his jaw, an exquisite pang shot through his face and turned against his brain. His jaw had been broken by that last terrible blow. The agony made him white, and he closed his eyes.

As for Dunleven, sitting there on his horse and watching with a savage curiosity, he made the grand mistake of his life in believing that the wincing and the pallor of the large man were caused by a sudden failing of nerve at the critical moment. Indeed, it was perhaps excusable to imagine that even a fighting Englishman would not wish to rise again to face the terrible battering of The Duke's hard fists. However, Dunleven had been trailed often enough by this old enemy. And now he should have known better.

He did not wait for a second thought, but, wheeling his horse away, he rode blithely down the trail, telling himself that the spirit of the ranger had been broken at last.

However, it is not the habit of Texas Rangers to have their spirits broken. They are made of a metal that may bend under stress but that will not break. And of all the rangers, John Tipton was the last to flinch. He made no effort to start up and call back his foe with a sharp challenge. He knew the thought that was in the brain of his enemy, but, after all, it was not the opinions of others that mattered to John Tipton. What counted to him was the voice of his conscience.

This day, then, went to Hubert Dunleven. But another day would come, God willing. In the meantime, there was no haste. This was merely another chapter in a story that had been spread over many years, and the word *Finis* had not yet been written.

Tipton tied a sling bandage around his face, and he rode to the nearest doctor.

When he recovered, he began again with his preparations. His captain made few demands upon the time of the ranger. He knew, and the whole band knew, that John Tipton had consecrated his life cheerfully and calmly to the work of apprehending that master criminal, Dunleven. And if the task were ever accomplished, it would be more than enough for Tipton, and would shed an additional luster over the entire band.

Only one thing was known above all else—that Tipton would and could not be hurried. Made as he was, of oak and iron, haste was not his way. He began again in his great labor as though half of eternity lay before him. Behind him lay the long generations of the service of the law that was bred into his bone, just as behind Dunleven lay long generations of defiance of the law—successful defiance, because the brilliant record of the Dunlevens had never been marred by any long terms spent in prison.

John Tipton was the ideal foxhound, but Dunleven was the ideal fox, with just a dash of tiger thrown in. To assist John Tipton, there were all the elaborate cogs of the machine of the law. Railroads, telegraph, a thousand helping hands would carry him on his way and do his bidding. But Dunleven had only himself. Perhaps the dash of tiger that was in him made it a drawn game.

At any rate, what Tipton did first of all was to take a long trip through the mountains—to recuperate from the fatigues of long labors read his furlough. As a matter of fact, he wanted only a chance to work up his hand with rifle and with revolver. If his back were to the wall, he would fight with bare hands. But after the last encounter, he knew that at rough and tumble he had met his master. Therefore, he turned to guns. Practice will make perfect, and John Tipton invested three months of daily labor with rifle and Colt.

When he came down from the mountains, he was a little thinner, his lips were compressed in a tensed line. Body and brain, he was under a nerve strain from long and delicate labors.

Then he picked up the tangled skein of the wanderings of Dunleven and labored for another three months before he came upon fresh traces.

That was in Arizona, where a bank had been blown open and the work done with a peculiar neatness and precision which, it seemed to the ranger, were typical of Dunleven. So he hastened to the spot. Yes, someone had seen, a few days before the robbery, a short, heavily-built man, with a long, elastic step.

That was enough. It answered the description of Dunleven, and it raised the heat of John Tipton. He cut for sign, and on the third day he reached a hint. It carried him north and east. He took a railroad, and got to Denver.

It was not the city that it is now, but it was a large place to spot a quarry such as Dunleven. There was no sign of him there, and Tipton worked outward from the city.

So, riding wearily toward the lights of a cross-roads mountain town, one evening, he came upon a little village perched at a perilous angle, as though about to slide down to ruin in the gulch beneath. He came to the hotel, and, riding around toward the rear of it, he paused opposite a window.

For through that open window he had just heard a voice saying: "I'll see that and raise you another ten, sir."

A curiously deep, smooth voice, with a metallic undertone in it that stopped the ranger like a reaching hand. He reined in closer to the window, and, leaning from the saddle, he looked straight into the eyes of his arch-enemy.

The darkness in which the ranger stood shielded him from the observation of the other, but exactly opposite to him was none other than Dunleven in the act of pushing a little stack of chips toward the center of the table.

Four other men sat around that table. They were all mountaineers of a grand and picturesque type—hardy adventurers, all with filled wallets. Perhaps not one of the lot had hands that were altogether clean.

For this was a serious game. The chips were stacked high, and their values were great. Honest men, perhaps, never had that much money to risk on such work—not honest men who dressed as roughly as these.

Indeed, to a casual eye, Dunleven was the least remarkable of all the persons there. He sat boyishly short in his chair, but that gave his shoulders an almost ludicrous width in contrast with his height. His swarthy face was pale. And the black eyes that the big ranger knew so well were oddly dull, as though a little film had been drawn across them.

However, it was the hands that fascinated Tipton most. He had never before, he thought, seen those hands so clearly as he did on this night. He had never before had an opportunity to find their character revealed. The hair grew down a little over their backs. Those hands were very bony, long of finger, and the thumbs bent back at the first joint, and yet seemed as strongly prehensile as the hands of a great ape.

John Tipton, watching those hands as the chips were fingered and then thrust out, felt a little quiver of apprehension pass through him. Once, in his youth, the tips of those fingers had been fixed on his throat. Tipton drew a deep breath. It was very good, indeed, to be still alive.

No doubt more than one man would have ridden straight up to the window and, leveling his rifle through it, have commanded the others in the room to take the fugitive from justice by force of numbers, but that was not what Tipton wanted. Mass action would satisfy the law. But in this matter, Tipton felt that he had a right to make some discrimination. In a sense, he was a mere servant of the law, but, in another sense, he was to be allowed to suit his own convenience.

He chose to stand face to face with the famous outlaw when he made that capture.

Yet he hesitated to move. If he rode around to the front of the hotel and entered from that direction, perhaps it would be difficult to make an entrance into this little room, and he feared to take his glance for an instant from the face of Dunleven.

At last, Hubert Dunleven raised his head with a start, and canted it a little to one side, and the eyes that he raised upon the open window had a fine gleam of light rising from their depths.

"Just lean back there and draw the shade across that window, Blondy," said Dunleven. "There's no good reason why the world and his wife should watch our game, eh?"

A long arm stretched back, and the shade came down with a screech and a rattle.

So the ranger, perforce, turned away, and he turned with a shiver. Of course, it was absurd to say that a man could see in the deep black of the night. But Dunleven possessed something almost as valuable as such an uncanny power—he had a guardian instinct that had warned him vaguely, subtly, that there was danger watching him from the heart of the night.

"All right, Jerry," said a big voice with a snarl in it. "Maybe that shade being drawn will change our luck. Deal again!"

"No," said the voice of Dunleven, "I've had enough!"

Chapter Three

"A SHOT THAT TOLD"

The ranger fled for the front of the hotel. The last announcement was enough to make him hurry. An instant more, and the grand opportunity might be lost, and forever.

He leaped from his mustang in front of the hotel, and, as he plunged up the front steps, he saw from the corner of his eye a splendid bay mare with ample quarters to carry weight and with a fineness of line that indicated superb speed.

Of course, he could not say that he recognized the horse of Dunleven. But one did not expect to find such a horse in a jerkwater mountain town—and it was just such an animal as the discerning eye of Dunleven would have selected, and the ample purse of Dunleven would have afforded.

This was the detail that he jotted down in his inner consciousness as he hurried into the hotel.

"Hello!" said the proprietor, heaving himself up with a suspicious face from behind his newspaper. "Hello," he repeated, passing a thumb under his single suspender and scowling at the hurrying form of the ranger: "What you might be wanting, stranger?"

Fellows of that type never liked big Tipton. There was something about the man of the law that looked so well-washed, both body and soul, that it put crafty rascals and greasy villains out of sorts with themselves.

"I want Jerry, and I want him in a hurry," said the ranger.

"You want Jerry, do you?" said the proprietor. "Oh,

maybe you're his cousin?"

"Has he got a cousin?" said John Tipton carelessly. "I don't know anything about that. I know that I want Jerry . . . will you show me where he is?"

"Humph," said the proprietor, "you talk as if you might know him, after all. Where would you *expect* to find him?"

"That depends," said Tipton. "But if there's a card game running in this place, he'll probably be there."

At that, the brows of the other raised, and he grinned broadly. "I guess you're all right," he said. "I'll take a chance on you, stranger." He hooked a thumb over his shoulder. "Go down the hall, yonder, and knock at the last door, straight ahead of you."

So John Tipton strode down the hall, conscious of the comfortable weight of the Colt at his hip, and, as he walked, he made a sort of silent prayer that this might be the last battle of all, and that out of it he might either secure the criminal, dead or alive, or leave his own dead body to mark the end of the fray.

When he came before the indicated door, he heard angry voices declaring: "You've made your clean-up, and now you want to draw out on us!"

To which the calm, steady voice of Dunleven made answer: "I warned you before I sat in at the game that I would leave when I felt like it, whether I were ahead or behind."

"Sure," said another. "We never figured that a white man would want to pull out when he had most of the cash in his pocket! Nobody ever heard of a thing like that! If you want to beat it, put the money back in the game!"

John Tipton braced himself a little. For at this point he expected a crash and an exceedingly loud one. In the old days that tigerish Dunleven would never have endured such talk from any man. However, it seemed that the new Dunleven was able to endure a great deal.

He merely said after a quiet moment: "I'll tell you what I'll do . . . I'll stake every penny that I've taken from the game on one roll of the dice. Does that sound to you?"

A moment of silence followed this daring proposal.

"Speak up," said Hubert Dunleven. "Time means a good deal to me, just now. I can't waste it, standing here, while you whisper together. Do you want to pool the coin and shake dice for the whole of it?"

Tipton felt a chill rising in his blood. By what uncanny powers of intuition had the big man been able to guess that a vital danger was approaching him? So sure an intuition that he would have been gone before this if these companions had not detained him.

"We'll let the game go on," answered one of the other gamblers sullenly. "We ain't been playing a dice game, and we ain't gonna turn it into a dice game now. Poker is the thing, stranger, and you're gonna sit down for another couple of hours until this here game has had a fair and square chance to work itself out. . . ."

"Very well," said Dunleven quietly, "if that's the way you feel about it . . . I'll have to make a change. . . ."

In spite of that quietness, he must have been preparing for swift and violent action. For now there was a sudden outbreak of turmoil in the room. Something crashed. The rim of light around the door went out as the lamp was extinguished. Immediately, through the dark which must have flooded the cardroom, came a cry.

"Guard the door! Watch that door, boys! He's got to go that way!" someone was shouting.

But here came a sudden tinkling sound of breaking glass.

"The window!"

Aye, Tipton had guessed that before and had stood in a quandary.

He wrenched the door open in time to see, against the dim stars beyond, a crowd of men lurching for the window, and shooting through it.

But a good general, in time of doubt, will strike at the communications of an enemy into contact with whom he cannot come. So Tipton whirled about without a word and raced down the hall and through the lobby, where all was commotion.

"Stop that tall gent!" yelled the proprietor. "The shooting started after he went down there . . . he's been gunning for Jerry, and most likely he's killed him. Hold up, big fellow, or we'll fill you full of lead! Dive for him, boys!"

The "boys" were three or four sturdy cowpunchers, and they flung themselves in a flying wedge at Tipton. A pile-driving blow with his long right broke the point off that wedge, and a hammering left stunned the second man and dropped him in his tracks. As for the third combatant, he had grappled hard with big Tipton, but the ranger picked him up as though he had been a child and flung him at the proprietor.

This delay, then, had been only a matter of seconds, and, leaving the floor of the little lobby strewed with writhing, groaning, cursing men, Tipton lurched for the door and reached it—in time to see an active form leap to the saddle on the bay and dart off into the night.

There was not much time. From the front of the hotel, a dim battery of lights played into the darkness, and Tipton had that brief distance of light in which to snatch out his Colt and fire—while the bay mare was leaping like a racer for the margin of blackness and safety.

He made that snap shot with speed and precision. Even as he pulled the trigger, he knew that it was a hit—and then he saw the form of Dunleven sag forward upon the neck of the horse.

He himself was instantly in the saddle upon his own mount. But he had ridden far in that day, and his weight was a crushing impost upon all except born weight carriers. The bay drew easily and swiftly away from him, and he was pumping lead vainly after a dancing shadow.

Others rode behind him, but they had started too late, and they were soon discouraged.

But though distanced, Tipton did not surrender. If he could not win by actual speed, yet he felt that he would be able to keep within striking distance—and he had before him a wounded man. Loss of blood would tell, in a long race.

So the ranger drew back his horse to a steady canter. The road was muffled with inches of velvet dust. There was only a dulled thrumming of the hoofs, and the sound of the water that the horse had drunk at the hotel trough sloshing up and down in his belly. He grunted a little with almost every stride. Certainly this night work was not to the taste of the mustang, but Tipton was without mercy. Ahead of him he felt that the goal of his labors lay ready at his hand.

The moon rose, and, as he came to the crest of a gentle rise, he saw a long, long stretch of the valley road gleaming for white miles before him, until it drove away out of view in the moon mist. And there was no sign of a horseman along its course.

So Tipton drew rein and looked thoughtfully around him.

He was both pleased and sorry. He was pleased, of course, because this was the surest token he could have asked that the wound of the bandit was deep and serious. Otherwise, with such a fleet horse beneath him, gaining with every stride that it took, what more could Dunleven have asked than such a straight road as this to carry him far, far away from his enemy?

No, Dunleven, badly hurt, had turned from the road to give his hurt the proper care, and perhaps he would even have become so weak that it would be necessary for him to rest for long hours.

At any rate, this was the first victorious point for the ranger. But the difficulty that went along with it was that all around him there was a tangle of big trees and little lanes that cut off through these trees, hither and yon—bridle paths leading to mountain trails, or blind alleys pointed straight at some farmhouse, perhaps. And there was only the night to search this wilderness.

No doubt few men would even have dreamed of attempting such work at such a time. They would have ridden post-haste back to the town. They would have raised an alarm, gathered a crowd, and swept the countryside, but Tipton had no confidence in mass proceedings. The larger the net, the greater the interstices, he had noted over and over again.

Beginning at the point where he had lost view of the fugitive, he began quietly to cut for sign.

Chapter Four

"A CUT FINGER"

He came, at length, upon a glimmering of light far before him, as he rode in circles of increasing size, with a dying hope in his heart. That single ray of light was rose-colored, at first. As he drew near, it appeared and disappeared before him, with every rise and fall of the ground over which he was traveling. When the sifting tree-trunks intervened, it winked like an uneasy star.

But at length, the ranger came out in front of a little cabin, with the kitchen door open, and the lamplight streaming far off among the forest trees.

He circled that cabin, front and back. He stalked to a window and looked in on a girl of twenty, or so, very busy in the washing of dishes, and singing softly at her work. The air was fragrant with the perfume of food, and suddenly John Tipton knew that he had not eaten since the early morning, and, besides, it was clear that a girl would not be singing idly and happily in the kitchen, if a dreaded desperado, a wounded man, were in the house.

So Tipson went boldly up to the kitchen door and tapped at it. "Hello!" he called out.

The girl whirled like one shot through the heart.

"What? What?" said John Tipton, taking off his hat. "Did I frighten you?"

"Not a bit," answered the girl. And she tried to smile, but made rather a bad job of it.

It occurred to Tipton that the door had been left open to

signal the way to some other person, and perhaps that was the reason that the girl was so frightened.

He nodded at her as reassuringly as he could. "If you're alone here," he said, "I don't want to bother you. Only I'd like to get a bite to eat, if I may, and then I'll jog on. . . ."

Here his eye passed to the table. It was cleared of the dishes with which it had been covered, with the exception of two cups and two saucers. The girl saw the direction of his glance.

"My father lives here with me," she said. "He's stepped out for a mite, but he'll be back again directly. And supper . . . of course, you can have that."

She tried to make it hearty, but it seemed to Tipton that she was only able to bring out the words with an effort. Hospitality she dared not refuse to him. For to refuse food to the hungry is a crime in every frontier land, and in the mountain desert more than in all other places.

However, he did not pause to consider in detail everything that she was saying and the inferences that might be gathered from the tone of her speech. What was of importance was that the girl had a father, and therefore, since she was not alone, he, Tipton, could spend the night on the place. That was what he wanted. He was very tired. He looked forward with dread to the thought of rambling on through the cold and the damp of the open air, and finally making himself an outdoor camp.

Therefore, while the major half of the invitation remained unspoken, he smiled and nodded at her again.

"All right," he said. "If you're expecting your father back, I'll just put up my horse in the shed, yonder, and be right in. Don't bother about fixing up a fancy feed for me. Cold pone and a slice of bacon and a cup of coffee will be fine."

And, with another smile, he stepped off to lead his horse

toward the shed. He remembered, then, that it would be an excellent thing to give his tired mount a feed of grain, if that were possible. So he stepped back to the door to ask the girl if there were either oats or barley.

What he saw was a thing that made a stir of trouble rise in the mind of Tipton. For the girl was standing in the middle of the floor, making no movement to prepare his lunch for him, and with head raised, she was staring at the trap that opened in the middle of the ceiling above her head. The ladder that was used to reach it lay, flatling, along one side of the room.

There is not much in such a gesture and such an attitude, perhaps, but John Tipton carried with him a mind that was trained to suspicion. He and his father and his forefathers before them had learned generation by generation the old, old lesson that things are often not what they seem. And now this tensed form of the girl, and the raised head that was directed toward the open trap, aroused an instant suspicion in him.

He turned and went slowly back toward the shed, with his question about the grain unasked. He was in a black humor, indeed. But it occurred to John Tipton that he had never before seen a girl so clear-eyed, so simple, and so gentle as she who was in the house behind him. Yet the ugly suspicion was firmly rooted in his mind that she was harboring another man in that house.

Aye, it was not for any father that she had set out the second coffee cup. Who, then? Why, when a girl was at that age, and, when she had an eye so richly blue, a smile so instant and so charming, she was bound to draw young fellows about her as honey draws the bees. So thought John Tipton. And he remembered, with an ache of the heart, that he himself was not so very old, and yet his roving life made it impossible for him to settle down and build a home.

He fell into a melancholy humor as he stripped the saddle from his horse and began to rub it down with dry wisps of hay. Of course, it was easy to see what had happened. The noise that his horse had made in approaching the cabin had startled the pair. The youth had scampered up the ladder into the loft, and the girl had hastily removed that same ladder and laid it by the wall. She had barely got back to the sink where she pretended to be busying herself with the work of cleaning the dishes, when the voice of Tipton sounded at her door. The fear and excitement that he had seen in her face had these ample explanations, he felt.

Well, this was no business of his. If she chose to entangle her young life with that of a man—guiltily entangle it, perhaps—he had no right to interfere. He was no sparrow hawk to fly at such small game, but an eagle towering in pride of place to strike down mighty ill-doers. The great Dunleven was his quarry, and none other interested him.

A horse stamped on the farther side of the shed, and he stepped to the side of it. When he laid his hand upon it, the hide was wet with sweat under his touch, and a steam of pungent vapors rose from the animal. He scratched a match to take a better look at the horse. But a guttering wind that pried through the crevices of the shed knocked out the flame of the match and played the same trick with still another.

He did not attempt to make a third trial. The matter did not seem of enough importance, and so he went back to the cabin. He found that his meal was in rapid course of preparation. He sat at the little deal table at the side of the room while an enameled iron plate was placed before him.

"My name is John Tipton," he said, by way of introduction.

"I am Nell Wooster," said the girl, busy decanting a quantity of brown baked beans from a great iron pot at the back of the stove.

"Hello!" exclaimed John Tipton, springing up. "What might this be?"

For as he turned his head he saw the lamplight falling strongly upon the floor, and in that flood of light there was a scattering of little round red stains soaked into the wood. Tipton dropped to his knees beside the spot and rubbed his thumb strongly against the place.

And the skin came away smudged across with red!

"Fresh! A fresh stain!" said Tipton. "What could have made this, Miss Wooster?"

He stood up and looked hard at her.

She was turning toward him from the stove, with a steam of cookery blown across her busy face.

"What's wrong, Mister Tipton?"

"I wondered what made this?" asked Tipton, fixing his sharp eye on her.

"Ah?" said she, "you mean the blood on the floor?"

He nodded, and it seemed to him that she paled a little and compressed her lips.

She explained: "I gave myself a nasty cut with the butcher knife a moment ago." She extended toward him a finger wrapped in a twist of white cloth; the cloth was reddening rapidly from the inside, even now.

It seemed very strange, indeed, to Tipton. His trained eye was not supposed to miss such details as this. And he felt that he could almost have sworn that the hands that, a little moment before, had been busy at the stove, had not been troubled by any bandage, no matter how small. However, he was tired, and he knew that a tired mind and a tired eye are rarely accurate.

He asked her to let him see it, for a vague suspicion had

formed in his mind. She was ready enough, however, at that. And, unwinding the bandage, she showed him a deep incision in her forefinger, with the blood springing readily up from the lips of the cut, the instant that the bandage was removed. The suspicion died away in the mind of the ranger.

But he showed his skill in making a new bandage with neat, narrow strips, and so winding them that all bleeding stopped, and yet the circulation of blood in the finger was not checked. After that, he was seated at the table, and the food was heaped high upon his plate.

Who can keep suspicion of the very hand that serves at the table? Not a man as hungry as John Tipton, no matter how keen his native good sense might be. He ate and he drank, and comfortable warmth flowed into his body and comfortable warmth flowed into his heart. And a veil was brushed suddenly from his eyes, and he saw in Nell Wooster a character, indeed, above suspicion, and a brown-skinned beauty such as he had never seen before in all his days.

Chapter Five

" 'IF YOU VALUE YOUR LIFE . . . ' "

Nell Wooster, as he started on a thick, handsome wedge of pumpkin pie, left the cottage with a pail in her hand, bound for the well, she told him. He would have taken the pail from her to run this errand, but she put it resolutely behind her and shook her head. He could never find it in the dark, and with so many rocks and roots and shrubs to stumble over.

So he saw her vanish through the doorway into the black of the night, and heard the faint creaking of the pail handle as she went swinging down the path. The heart of the ranger went strongly after her. He forgot his food—but only for a moment.

The rest of the pumpkin pie disappeared. The coffee was swallowed, and, as John Tipton crammed the bowl of his pipe to fullness, he cast his swift and accurate eye around the cabin. First he counted the guns in the rifle rack at the farther corner and admired the way the light glanced across their well-oiled and polished surfaces. The man of this house was obviously one who took most expert care of his weapons. And such a point meant a great deal to Tipton, whose guns were like a portion of his own flesh.

Then he observed the whiteness of the floor. Nothing but many scrubbings with soap and steaming hot water could produce that color, as he very well knew. Drops of blood might readily be lost in the general dinginess of the floor of the average mountain cabin. But against this spotless whiteness, they stood out in a bold relief.

The heart of the ranger swelled with satisfaction. The daughter of no Devon farmer, even of the neat-handed housewives around Barnstaple, could have showed a more laudable and patient industry. Again a rush of warmth passed dizzily into his brain.

He tried to push the tender sentiment away from him, for he told himself that a man on a blood trail must never be moved by his personal affairs. All that existed of John Tipton, at this moment, should belong to the state that paid him his wages. However, nature was working strong, strongly in his bosom.

He surveyed the pots that ranged the section of the room around the stove, and they, too, had been scrubbed with sand until they shone like translucent things instead of stubborn iron and copper. Once more the woman's hand.

Aye, all that he saw were tokens to him of self-respecting and honest frontier people. But the old question leaped back into his mind. Why, after his coming, had the girl showed such fear and excitement? And why, when he slipped back to the door, had he found her with her head raised to inspect the trap door that opened upon the attic above the room?

Tipton raised his own leonine head and stared at the black rectangle. It might be nothing, and again it might be everything. To be caught in the act of investigating the house of his host would be a shameful thing. And yet—would not the creaking of the bail of the bucket give him ample warning of the approach of the girl?

He had no sooner made that decision than a violent curiosity beat down all scruples. He picked up the ladder at the side of the room and placed it hastily in position with the top edge of the poles resting against the trap. Then he started mounting.

He had not climbed two rungs when he heard a dry, quiet voice saying behind him: "Well, stranger, I hope that you're makin' yourself at home, here?"

He jerked his head over his shoulder, and there he saw a tall, thin, gray-haired man dressed in a tattered, leather coat, with a leather hunting hat settled low above his eyes. Over his shoulder there was borne a big canvas sack, perhaps crammed with game, but, most significant of all to the man up the ladder, the new arrival bore a shotgun that was dropped into the crook of the left arm and, with the right finger upon the trigger, carefully covered the ranger.

John Tipton made no mistake. He did not loiter upon the ladder. Neither did he leap down in too much haste. But he was more than a little red as he turned and faced the man with the shotgun.

"I don't know who you be," said the gray-headed man.

"He is John Tipton, Dad," said the voice of Nell Wooster from the rear of the tall man. "And I'm sure that he's all right."

"All right, is he?" responded Wooster. "Then what's he doing climbing the ladder to the attic?"

"Oh!" gasped the girl. "Was he doing that?"

She stepped into the view of Tipton. There was no bucket in her hand, and the ranger felt that he could understand why that was. On the way to the well she had met her father, and she had come hastily home with him and left the bucket behind.

But the surprise and the anger with which she was studying him now made Tipton wince. It was not in this manner that honest folk were in the habit of regarding him.

"I heard a noise up there," said Tipton. "And I thought that I would investigate it."

The hunter smiled and nodded in sardonic agreement.

"Something creaked, eh? Like a mouse or a man, perhaps?"

Tipton flushed more deeply than before. It was not the contempt of the man that he minded so much, but the open contempt in the face of the girl was a scourge to him.

"Mister Wooster," he said, "I would like to. . . ."

"One minute!" snapped Wooster. "You just keep those hands of yours away from your hips, will you? I like you fine, stranger. But while you're here with me, you mind your step. I ain't here to take chances with gents like you. Just hoist up those hands of yours, will you? Nell, you go through his clothes and take any guns that he may have handy around him. This here gent looks like a mighty suspicious one to me."

"Dad," said the girl, her eyes still fixed on the open face of the man from Devon, "are you sure that he ought to be searched?"

"Are you old enough and smart enough to know more than your dad?" snapped Wooster. "Go do what I tell you to do, and hurry along about it. Tipton, mind them hands of yours!"

He had a veritable look of murder in his eyes as he spoke, and Tipton raised his hands well above the level of his shoulders while the girl took away the heavy Colt at his hip. Next she located the two weapons slung next to his skin beneath his shirt.

They were produced to the almost savage satisfaction of Wooster.

"We're getting down to the truth about this," he stated. "Three guns is more than any honest man needs to wear. Tipton, you get your shoulders back against that wall and shove them hands well up above your head."

Tipton was cooler now. There was sufficient danger here to make him forget such a petty thing as embarrassment. So he stepped back quietly until his shoulders rested against the smoothly adzed inner surface of the log wall. There he waited.

"Now," said the hunter, keeping the gun leveled at the breast of the ranger, "what you got to offer? Are you one of these here gunfighters or ain't you?"

"In my business," said Tipton, "we have to travel well-heeled."

"And what might that business be?" sneered the other. "Are the kind of cows that you punch in your section of the range that dangerous?"

"I don't punch cows," said Tipton.

"No, you don't. And you don't work in the woods, and you don't mine, either. What's your game, young feller?"

"I'm working for the State of Texas," said Tipton, "as a ranger."

"As a what?" snapped the other.

But the girl understood first with a gasped: "A Texas Ranger, Dad! I knew that he was honest!"

"A Texas Ranger," repeated Wooster, as the name of that famous organization came home to him. "Why, that would sort of change things, I suppose. Have you got a commission on you?"

"I have."

"Let's have a look at it."

It was passed to Wooster, and he examined it with keen attention. He refolded it and passed it back. The formidable shotgun the next instant came with a *thump* to the floor.

"Well," he said, "give him back his guns. Tipton, if that's your name, I'm sorry that I mistook you. But I've got one grudge against the world, and that's a grudge at every sneaking coyote that wears more guns than he needs to bring down game. A grudge, Ranger, ag'in' every damn' rat that practices up ways of putting lead into the hides of honest men. Y'understand me? I come West when things was wild and woolly. I seen the badmen when they *were* bad, and I've hated and despised the lot of them ever since. But a fellow like you, Tipton, doing the business that the rangers do . . . why, it's like meeting a brother."

He extended a hand as hard as tanned leather, and Tipton took it willingly enough. He put away his weapons.

"As far as what's in the loft," said Wooster, "you're welcome to take as long a look as you want. Go up the ladder, Tipton, though I dunno what sort of a noise that you could've heard up there." He turned toward the door. "I got to get in a mite of wood," he explained. "I'll be right back." And he stepped out into the night.

As for Tipton, he wanted no second invitation. He merely cast one apologetic look at the girl, and then he began to mount the ladder. But when his hand was reaching for the topmost rung and his head was close to the black shadow of the trap, he heard a gasping voice from the girl and turned in haste to look at her. She had clasped her hands across her breast, and her face was white.

"Don't go another step," she breathed to him. "If you value your life, don't go another step."

Chapter Six

"THE PUZZLE"

There was not so little imagination in the ranger that he had to ask the girl to explain her meaning. He promptly descended the ladder, and, stepping as far as possible from beneath the yawning mouth of the trap above him, he stood before Nell Wooster. He came directly and suddenly to the point: "Now, Miss Wooster," he began, "I want to know who was apt to hold a gun at my head, if you please?"

"I said nothing about a gun," answered poor Nell, shrinking from him.

The ranger pointed over his head toward the yawning trap.

"There's someone in that loft," he said, "and I won't try to make you tell me who he is. Only . . . we haven't given him half a chance to get away from the house. Tell me . . . is he a man that I'd want to see . . . or it is just your lover, Nell, who hid himself away when you heard my horse coming toward your house. Will you tell me what is what?"

There was still another possibility, and he was turning it slowly in his mind. The blood on the floor—the man in the loft—the sweating horse in the shed—might they not point toward something of more importance than a mere foolish lover who hid himself away from the eye of the world, conscious of his guilt? Might these tokens not indicate that a fugitive from justice was yonder in the garret? If that were the case, of course, it could be only one man—it was the great

137

Dunleven and no other man.

So, as the thought entered the mind of the ranger, an electric thrill passed to his very soul. It was true that the girl was pretty and her fear was touching, and certainly, if Dunleven were hidden in the loft, then her warning had saved the life of his pursuer. Yet, none of these factors would have weighed for an instant with John Tipton. Aye, for even a man's sweetheart will not stand between him and his lifework, if he is the right manner of man. John Tipton was distinctly the right type, and the capture of Dunleven was assuredly his lifework.

However, just because the suspicion that it might be Dunleven entered his head, he did not for that reason come to any rash decisions. First of all, he considered the whole case with a meticulous care. Dunleven was not the sort of a man who would trust himself to a woman, and particularly to a clean-eyed girl of this type. In the second place, if this girl had such a person as the famous Dunleven in her house, she would never have been able to keep a face even as well as she had done. In the third place, and what was most decisive in the opinion of the ranger, Wooster himself was a man who loved law and hated gunfighters, and, being reared in such a school, Nell would not be apt to have much sympathy for such a reprobate as Dunleven.

So, considering all these matters through a course of seconds, John Tipton decided against pressing a search of the loft unless he got further items to arouse his suspicions. Moreover, as he faced the girl and watched her, he saw her grow a most fiery red.

"I . . . I don't quite understand you, Mister Tipton," she said, and grew more furiously red than ever.

John Tipton was more than two-thirds decided, on the spot. However, he wished to make assurance doubly sure.

"I think you *do* understand," he said, and he smiled down into her eyes with his own honest blue ones—true Tipton blue, such as had looked down gun barrels through these many generations, striking terror and awe into the hearts of ill-doers. "You do understand. I'm a law officer, Nell. And yonder there's a man that you're hiding. That's plain, isn't it?"

She swallowed, blinked, and faced him again. "Yes!" gasped Nell.

"Very well, then, that fellow is either a fugitive from law, and, therefore, I should have him . . . or else he's a gentleman who doesn't care to have it known that he's . . . courting Nell Wooster, let's put it. Now, will you give me your word of honor that it is not a man I should see?"

"Yes," said the girl without a moment's hesitation. "Of course, I'll give you my word of honor. Heavens, Mister Tipton, what would I be doing to . . . ?"

"Very well," said Tipton, "I believe you."

And he did. For she had faced him so squarely and spoken so bravely to him that it was impossible for him to doubt her. He had not much experience with women. He was one of that type of men who feel an unquieting interest in the other sex only when they have decided that it is time to settle down and make a home. These fellows are honorable by instinct rather than by principle, and the books can only tell them what is already firmly in their natures and their inmost souls.

The complexion of this girl appeared as pink-and-white, and her eye was so tenderly clear, and her ear—ridiculous detail!—was so absurdly rosy, like the ear of an infant, that John Tipton decided that she was the very soul of holy integrity.

"I believe you," said Tipton, "but this matter is so important that I want you to reinforce that word of honor by taking my hand as you tell me that the man I want is not in your house."

"Ah?" said Nell Wooster. "You are after some dreadful man?"

John Tipton raised his head a little after the fashion of one who honestly does not wish to overstate. But then he said: "I'll tell you, in fact, that this is the cleverest and most daring rascal that ever rode through the mountain desert. A short man, with heavy wide shoulders and a long, elastic stride . . . you know?" He was quoting from the descriptions that were published far and wide of the outlaw. "Hubert Dunleven is the man that I want!"

"Dunleven!" gasped the girl. "Dunleven! Oh, I've heard something about him."

"I hope you have," said the ranger. "If you read the papers, or if you listen to what people have to say of each other . . . Dunleven? Yes, I suppose that everyone has heard tell of Dunleven."

"Aye, the black scoundrel!" exclaimed the heavy voice of Mr. Wooster, as he stamped into the house again. He gave his hat and his coat to his daughter and sat down in a corner. She knelt before him and began to unlace the high boots that he wore. And, from great weariness, his head fell back against the wall of the cabin, and his features relaxed as he stared at the ranger, and his eye lost some of its fire.

"Aye," he said, nodding, "we've all heard something about that Dunleven, I s'pose. Though I try to keep the girl, here, from wasting her mind thinking about such things. But he's the worst of them all, is Dunleven."

"The worst of them all?" breathed the girl. "The worst of them all? But what's he done?"

"Why," said her father, "what is there for a man to do that's wrong? What is there, beginning with murder and winding up with hellish theft and gambling and cheating devices? What is there? Dunleven has done it all! But you should be able to talk on that theme, Tipton. Tell us what Dunleven has done. I want my girl to know one picture of a badman."

"I'll tell you," said Tipton, smiling faintly. "Dunleven is everything except a thief, I suppose. . . ."

"Not a thief?" cried the hunter. "Not a thief? Then I've not been able to read print right, or else the papers have lied!"

"Well," said Tipton, "if you count what he's taken when he's in flight . . . yes, he's a thief."

"Little things like horses and saddles, and food and guns, and such things . . . that's what he's stolen, Tipton, and you know it! And what of the banks that he's broken into and blown the safes open . . . ?"

"True," said Tipton, "but I was referring to sneak thievery . . . picking pockets, or stealing into private houses by night . . . such things are beneath him. They're not dangerous enough."

"But," said Nell Wooster, "could one man break into a bank and . . . blow up the safe?"

"Aye," smiled Tipton, "such a man as Dunleven could, and has done more times than you have fingers and toes, Nell Wooster. My word on that!"

"Blows up the safes?" echoed the girl. "But how can he do it?"

"With nitroglycerin."

"What?" she cried. "When a single shake of the bottle might . . . ?"

"Blow him to heaven? Yes, but he used it to blow him into a good bank account, which is another way of saying the same thing, I suppose."

"How terribly brave he must be," sighed the girl, staring through the door at the blackness of the night.

"And he has done a good many other things," said the ranger. "Once he was tried for murder, but he was acquitted. There wasn't any doubt that he had killed his man, but, when Dunleven does a killing, he doesn't shoot from behind. He stands up face to face. That's better. That's braver. But just the same, it is a killing. Only . . . out here in the West juries don't like to hang a man for what they call self-defense. Otherwise, he's killed enough white men to deserve hanging half a dozen times. As for the Mexicans . . . why, no one knows all of the deviltry that he raises south of the Río Grande. We get only echoes of it, on this side of the river, from time to time."

He smiled blandly on them. Wooster himself, breaking into a furious denunciation on his favorite theme, strode up and down the room in the soft slippers with which his daughter had equipped his feet, but Nell remained at a stand, staring through the door at the witchery of the open night, as though she were seeing new stars born into the shadow of the sky, one by one.

"Does he have no friends?" she asked at last.

"He rides too fast to gather moss," said the ranger. "And that's his strength. There are no friends to betray him."

"But how sad," said Nell Wooster. "Oh, how very sad."

Chapter Seven

"THE WOUNDED MAN"

That night, big John Tipton slept in an extra bunk in the room of his host. The next morning, he took his horse and rode away. There was no sign of any animal in the horse shed or in the pasture bearing a sweat-crusted coat, streaked with salt—such as must have been on the steaming horse that he had stood beside in the shed the night before.

But he merely smiled at this. Of course, the girl had been too shrewd to let the beast remain in the shed until the arrival of her father. Her lover had slipped down from the loft during the night, and now he rode far away through the woods, perhaps cursing the luckless arrival of a ranger that had sent him into such disagreeable hiding.

In the meantime, there was work—and long work—before John Tipton. His horse had been freshened by the rest and the good hay. He himself was cheered by good food and long sleep. As John Tipton reined his horse on the ridge of the next hill, he felt that he had every reason for feeling himself happier than ever before in his life. Here he was, fit and well and strong, and somewhere, surely not far off, in this very neighborhood, must be lying the wounded man, Dunleven.

Yet he was not gay. In spite of himself, he turned in the saddle and looked back to the little cabin of Jeremy Wooster with a pang of regret. Jeremy himself was striding away toward the woods with his game bag at his back, his rifle on his shoulder. He waved farewell cordially to the man of the law, and Tipton waved back. But the hunter was not the form in the eye of Tipton. His stare was fixed upon the form of the girl at the door of the cabin. She, too, waved, but it was a single perfunctory gesture. Tipton drew a long sigh.

If he had allowed himself the luxury of weakness, he would have become hopelessly sentimental in no time. But he ruled himself with a stern hand and allowed few of these lapses. Sentiment had to fight a stern battle and a long one before it could gain a hold upon the ranger. Now he turned his back and squared his shoulders at the cabin, and then he rode slowly off down the hill.

Nell Wooster watched him go. He was barely out of view, and her father was barely lost among the shadows at the edge of the forest, when Nell had caught up the heavy ladder at the side of the room and clapped it to the trap door in the ceiling. Up she ran, as light as a climbing cat, and then, crouched in the darkness of the loft, she called: "Hubert Dunleven!"

She waited as a stroke of fear almost stopped her heart. She was about to cry out again, as she scratched a match. But just as the light spurted at the end of the match, she heard a muffled yawn of prodigious dimensions. Then the flame of the match, clearing from sulphurous blue to yellow, showed her Hubert Dunleven rearing himself upon one elbow and making idle pretense of covering his yawn with one hand.

He sat up—a grizzly fiend in appearance. He was never lovely. Last night, in his blood and his weariness and his pain, he had seemed almost pathetic. That was before she had known who he was or the record that lay behind him. And now, with his hair on end, his eyes sunken, his face covered with a shag of unshaven beard, he appeared a veritable devil.

He smiled at her and waved his hand, and the girl shrank from the gesture. She had not noticed, the night before, how like the long arms and the wide shoulders of a gorilla were the arms and the shoulders of the fugitive.

The match died in a gust of wind. She was left in the semi-blackness of the loft and heard the monster stirring. Panic came upon Nell Wooster. She hurried for the ladder, but she missed the trap and floundered into great darkness. An hysterical confusion crossed her mind, blotting out all cool common sense. She cried out, and then she heard the scratching of a match, and there was a little spurt of flame.

There she saw the devil holding a light and grinning at her as he touched the flame of the match to the candle that she had put beside him here, the night before.

"There you are," said Dunleven. "That ought to give you light enough for running away, eh?"

The light, the calmness of his voice, and above all the sight of the stained bandages that wrapped his body acted to clear her mind again. She turned back to him, smiling and flushed.

"I'm sorry," said Nell Wooster. "I thought for a minute. . . ."

"Don't apologize," said Dunleven, and again he waved his gigantic arm airily. "Don't apologize. It's always been that way. I've always been so ugly that I've frightened the girls . . . and some of the boys, too." He grinned with a sardonic self-content at Nell.

It amazed her to hear him as much as it amazed her to see him. And suddenly she cried to him: "You were *not* desperately wounded last night when you came. It . . . it was a sham!"

"Sham?" said Dunleven, still grinning. "You saw the blood, didn't you?"

"Stuff," said the girl. "I got as much blood from my little finger. It *was* a sham. You were *not* afraid that you were dying."

"I was," said Dunleven. "But of weariness more than

wounds. That's the naked truth, if you'll have it. I was tired almost to death, Nell."

She put up her head at the familiarity in his tone. "If you know my name," she said, "I know yours, also."

"You will not speak it," he said. "You may know it, but you will never speak it, eh?"

"Why not?" frowned Nell.

"Because," he said, "well-bred little girls are taught not to call on the devil. Isn't that so?"

There was a good deal of iron in Nell Wooster, in spite of her mildness.

"You need not treat me like a child, Hubert Dunleven," she said.

He nodded, smiling at her. "Good," he said. "You are not afraid to say the name out loud. Hubert Dunleven! Hubert Dunleven! Do you know, my dear, that there are even a great many grown men and strong men who do not like to pronounce it carelessly? Believe me . . . for it is very true."

"Do you boast of it?" she asked.

"Yes. I boast of it. It pleases me. I love to be feared, my dear."

"Do not speak to me like this," said Nell Wooster, her dignity rising every moment. "I do not wish to be spoken to in this manner, Mister Dunleven."

"I cannot talk in any other," said Dunleven calmly. "For every person there is a proper tone. Some men must be talked to in pity, some in contempt, some in scorn, some in irony, some in good nature, some with indifference, some with gentleness, some in anger. Some men must be addressed with concern, some with amusement . . . some will have you speak bluntly, and some will have a veil thrown over everything that you speak. For each person in this world, there is an established tone that is proper to use upon him. And so there is for you only one proper tone, and that is the one which I am using at the present moment."

She grew so angry that the blood beat with a swift and aching throb in her temples. "And what is this tone, then?" asked Nell.

"My dear," said Dunleven, "the proper tone for you is one of affection and amusement, mingled with equal parts."

"What a detestable thing to say," breathed the girl.

"Not at all," he said, "if you have the patience and the intelligence to look at the matter with clear eyes. For you see that you are young and deliciously fresh and cool. . . ."

"I don't want to hear you!" cried Nell.

"You do, though," said Dunleven. "You don't like this patronizing manner, but you can't help enjoying this part of what I have to say. I say that you are really very pretty. Almost beautiful. Better than beautiful, to a person with proper taste. But, in addition to these charming qualities of person, you have courage, a child's curiosity, and a born honesty. All of these things are admirable. But on the other side of the picture must be written down a good deal of vanity, a good deal of self-assurance, and a habit of bearing a strong hand over a man because you have found that your pretty face is enough to make them all foolish around you."

He paused, and yawned, and Nell Wooster stood agape and dumb at such incredible assurance, such incredible effrontery. Never before had she encountered a man capable of speaking in this fashion.

"In the meantime," said the outlaw, "I am hungry as the very devil for which you mistook me, a while ago. But I cannot dine on human souls, as the devils are believed to do with such relish. As a matter of fact, I am not greatly interested in souls, even in yours, my pet. I have an incurable admiration of bacon and eggs, however. I know that you have bacon, and did I not hear a hen cackling behind the cabin, a little time ago?"

What she wished, at that moment, was that a whole company of rangers might rush in upon this cool demon. Then she would be able to see whether or not his poise would hold in the face of men.

She said: "If I were able to ride, and if I were you, I'd jump on my horse and gallop hard. Because a Texas Ranger was here on your trail, last night."

He nodded. "Dear old Tipton," he muttered. "Yes, I heard his voice. By the way, you have not answered me on the question of the eggs . . . ?"

"Confound the eggs!" cried Nell Wooster. "Aren't you . . . ?"

"Ashamed to be interested in such things? No dear. There is nothing dearer to my heart. Have you any eggs, for the third time?"

"Yes," said Nell, almost speechless.

"Then run along and cook them . . . a dozen of 'em, if you will. And, in the meantime, in honor of an egg breakfast, I'll clean up and scrape off this beard."

Chapter Eight

"A LITTLE STORY"

All the kindness and pity that the girl had felt for the stranger had left her before she hurried down the ladder from the loft; only a strict sense of duty to a stranger made her go sullenly ahead with the preparations for his breakfast. He seemed to take everything for granted, and that fact made her the more angry.

Presently he came down the ladder in turn, moving leisurely, and whistling softly as he climbed. He marched to the stove, found the steaming kettle of hot water, and poured out a quantity into a basin. Then he produced and unfolded a minute little shaving kit and, humming to himself, proceeded to shave with wonderful deftness and ease. Before the eggs and bacon and coffee had been prepared, he was ready and waiting. As she served him, she studied his long, lean face made ominous by the sunken eyes and the wide-boned jaw. She had thought that his unkempt ugliness could not be much improved upon; now that he was sleeked over, she thought him still more dreadful. The growth of hair on his face had served to mask some of its grimness. But now she could see the full truth about him, and that truth made her regret again that the clean-eyed, handsome ranger had not set his hands upon such a prize as this.

He ate his breakfast with dispatch, but still without apparent haste. Then he sat in a corner of the room and lighted a cigarette—not an honest wisp of brown paper filled by hand with yellow Bull Durham, but a "tailor-made" luxury from

Egypt that filled the cabin with a rich, strange fragrance. All this time, he did not speak, but he continually eyed her with calm appraisal.

At length he smiled at her, and said: "This odd-smelling smoke will air out. Your father will never have a breath of it. And as for myself, I'll be away in another moment or so. I only wish to sit here and chat with you a little more after breakfast. It's not good to hurry to work after eating, you know. Therefore . . . more talk, if you please."

"Have we been talking?" she asked him gloomily.

"A constant stream of comment and interchanging views," said the outlaw.

"I have not spoken a word for half an hour," she said.

"Ah, words?" he said. "Words are a small matter, my dear lady. A very small matter. Do you know that when good Indian warriors were on the war trail, they often went for whole weeks with hardly a word said? But they had signs. A sign language. And so have we civilized people . . . even when we least suspect it."

She stared at him vaguely, without comprehension.

"For instance," he explained, "there are your hands. Hands have an eloquence all their own. Your small brown ones, for example, have never before served a meal to a hungry man without enjoying their work. They have been gay and swift and tireless. They have carried dishes to every hungry table with a certain charming eagerness. And it has been a sad thing to sit here and to watch those hands working like slaves, heavily, joylessly, dragging themselves along."

"Slaves?" said the girl in anger. "How could they be slaves? Do you think that I have fed you because I am *afraid* of you, Hubert Dunleven?"

He canted his head upon one side and grinned quizzically up at her. "How you say that name," he commented. "There are three devils . . . Beelzebub, Belial, and Hubert Dunleven. The last a little the blackest of all the three. However, I did not really mean that you were a slave to fear. The master your poor hands have been obeying so sadly is called conscience . . . which makes cowards of us all, as someone says . . . I forget his name. Conscience is a bitter taskmaster, and it is conscience that has been berating you, and driving poor Nell Wooster to this work.

" 'I will not serve him!' says the honest brown hands.

" 'Yes,' says conscience, 'cook for him you must and shall, because he is a hungry, wounded, hunted man, and has three strong claims upon my hospitality.' "

He ended his whimsical speech, still shaking his head at her, and the girl drew back and watched him coldly.

"That's the sort of conversation that we've been holding," said Dunleven. "Looks, and attitudes, and gestures. Much more important than words. A man will lie with his words. But he cannot control the corners of his lips, or his eyes. The truth comes into them, if you have half an eye to read it. Shall I tell you a story about that?"

"If you wish to," said Nell Wooster.

"Tut, tut!" said the bandit. "You want me to be gone, I know. Nevertheless, this is a story that will interest even you. A very great deal, at that."

She shrugged her shoulders.

"It was the Thirteenth of September, and it was on Friday," he began. "A black Friday, you understand. And, like all criminals, of course, I'm superstitious. Can't help it, you know. The odd ideas will come jumping into the mind of a hunted man, and then he is as weak as a woman.

"However, on the morning of that day, a silly man decided that he would make himself famous, and so he tackled me. I didn't want him to harm him . . . but he insisted. I had to shoot, and the bullet traveled a whole span higher than I intended it to. I meant it for the hip. But it struck him in the body. A nasty wound! A horribly nasty wound, and there was no doctor near. And nobody around with half as much sense in the treatment of wounds as I possess myself. I wanted, really, to stay and dress that wound and try to pull the silly fool through. But I knew that, if I tried to stay, I'd be lynched. A crowd was up. Its temper was pretty high. And I decided that my life would be worth more to the world than that of my victim. You understand?"

"I hear what you say," said Nell bitterly. "I suppose he was an honest man?"

"He was, and is," said the outlaw. "He lived in spite of the bullet and more in spite of the fellows who tried to doctor him. However, I rode out of that camp convinced that there was a dying man behind me. In two hours, I was riding blind baggage . . . but when the train came into the first station, there was a crowd waiting. Too many guns in that crowd, I thought. They know something. And I ran over the tops of the cars before the train came to a stand and dropped off the rear platform. But some of them saw me and started for me. . . ."

"Heavens!" cried Nell.

"I thought the same thing," said the outlaw, grinning again. "But I managed to get around the first corner ahead of their bullets, and a minute later I was on the back of a horse. I rode that horse into the ground in an hour, borrowed a second out of a field. Changed that again in the middle of the afternoon, and in the evening I pulled into a mountain town rather fagged and hungry, because I hadn't slept more than a wink during the two nights that went before.

"Too tired to play safe, you understand? Should have cooked myself a snack among the trees, but there was a damp mist falling. I was half soaked, already. My stomach was empty. My matches were damp, too. I had nothing but bacon and flour to cook. I decided to risk going into the hotel in that little town and getting a made-to-order dinner. You understand?"

"Yes, yes!" said Nell Wooster. "I understand. And then? And then?"

"And then I did that very thing. I went into the town. I tied my horse to the hitching rack. I walked into the hotel, and in the lobby I warmed myself in front of the stove. Some of the men looked at me, but only because I looked wet and tired. Then I tried the dining room, and everything was easy.

"I sat there and ate a good steak while a conversation at the table next to mine described what I had done that morning and how I had been chased during the day. But they didn't dream of looking across their shoulders at me and sizing me up. I got down to coffee and had one hot cup under my belt and felt myself break out in a steam, when the talk at the next table shifted back a bit to the days when I had been doing something else. Then they began to talk about my ugly looks. In another minute the youngest fellow at that table looked across at me, and, from the corner of my eye, I saw him freeze.

"Yes, he had seen me and recognized me. The talk had brushed the mist from his eyes, at last, and now he was able to recognize that a handsome man-size reward for capture was sitting almost at his hand.

"But the bigness of the discovery was too much for him. He couldn't believe that he had really seen me. He wouldn't trust his eyes.

"However, I knew that in another minute he would tumble out of the cloud. I had to do something. If it was to make a sudden move to escape . . . why, no man is half so fast with his feet as others are with their guns. I couldn't run away."

"Then what *did* you do?" gasped the girl.

"Got up and walked away," grinned the devil in Hubert Dunleven. "I stood up and stretched and told the waiter to bring in another cup of hot coffee for me because I'd be back in a minute. Then I walked out of the room . . . and stopped near the door to admire a pair of elk horns hanging there. Just as I turned out of the door, the youngster came back to his wits and shouted . . . 'Hey, there . . . !' "

"And then?" gasped Nell Wooster.

"I just jumped sidewise through that door and sprinted. When I got to the front of the hotel, I didn't have any time to untie my horse. As a matter of fact, that horse was tired, anyway. Behind me, the boys were coming as fast as their boots would let them, and they were yelling that it was Dunleven and that the best job was to kill the fox and not try to capture him at all. Real wicked talk, eh?"

He stopped and threw back his ugly head and closed his eyes and laughed. She hated him as much as ever, but still she was so interested that she breathed: "But you *did* get away?"

"A young fool on a brand new saddle, in brand new clothes, on a brand new mare, and a beauty she was, rode around the corner of the hotel at that moment, and I dived for him. I had him out of the saddle in a jiffy and sat in his place, and so I scooted away into the thick of the dusk, with the bullets combing around me. But it takes good target work to nail a man on horseback moving at full speed . . . very good work . . . too good to expect from a Colt, you know."

"Ah!" breathed the girl. "What a dreadful thing!"

"I told you that," said Dunleven, "partly because I wanted to show off my good nerve and my quick thinking, I suppose. But partly, too, to tell you that full conversation can be made up of nothing more than gestures and looks. One look gave me a warning as clearly as the fall of a red flag. Just as the look in your eyes, at this moment, says perfectly clearly . . . 'Can such a monster ever have had a mother?' "

He brought the point back to her with such a start that she jumped and blinked at him again.

"Ah, well," said Dunleven, "here we are, the two of us, again."

"Again?" said the girl.

"I mean, the mare and I," said Dunleven.

"Ah," said Nell Wooster. "Do you mean to say that all of this happened only while you were fleeing here to . . . ?"

"Not at all. It was a long time ago. But when I came back this way, I remembered that mare, and, when I was in the need of a horse, I simply made a call . . . and found what I wanted. But you've seen for yourself, and she's a beauty, eh?"

Chapter Nine

"OF TIPTON"

He finished his cigarette and leaned forward to rise, but Nell stopped him.

"You talk about your horse and about things that you have done," she said, "but you don't speak about what matters most . . . your wound."

"That," said Hubert Dunleven, "is really nothing. There is only a graze along my side. It cost me a little blood and a little weakness . . . but, if it had not been that Tipton was after me, I should never have paused and I should have never, certainly, looked for shelter. But Tipton is no ordinary fellow. He is not even an ordinary ranger, and they're all an uncommon lot."

Nell shrugged her shoulders, decidedly unimpressed.

"You don't think much of him?" interpreted Dunleven.

"I've seen him and talked to him," said the girl.

"That's nothing," said Dunleven. "The vocabulary of a fellow like Tipton was never meant to express what he is. He is a great deal more than he seems, believe me. He can't look like anything other than a simple good fellow. And he can't talk like anything more than that, either. But Tipton in action is another matter. Quite another matter!"

"Are you afraid of him?"

"Afraid of him? I fear him as most men fear the devil! Afraid of him? He has brought me to the verge of hanging once, and to the very edge of the prison three more times, I

156

suppose. He has haunted my sleep for eight years. I dread him like poison!"

She shook her head.

"You don't believe me?"

"I don't believe you," said the girl.

"And why?"

"He's not so cunning," said Nell Wooster, as impersonally as her companion himself could have spoken. "And I'm sure that he isn't as clever with weapons. I know that he isn't even as strong, in spite of his size."

With her eyes, she scanned thoughtfully the wide shoulders and the terribly long, sinewy arms of the outlaw. The other was smiling and nodding at her, very well pleased.

"That's true . . . that's *very* true," he agreed. "Not so clever with guns or with wits, that friend Tipton of mine. Not quite as strong in the hands and the arms, either . . . though he comes terribly close to being. But he has something else that helps him against me."

"And what is that . . . the power of the law behind him?"

"Oh, that is something. It gives him extra hands to strike with, and longer arms. He can use the telephone and the telegraph to head me off. He has the power to call in help when it comes to a pinch. But the law is only a minor asset to Tipton. He has two other things that are huge advantages."

"I'd like to know them," Nell urged.

"In the first place," said the outlaw, "he has the advantage of hating me."

"Is that an advantage? Can't you hate him back just as hard?"

"Yes," murmured the other, in thought, "when I was a trifle younger I was able to hate him. But I have become too mature and too intelligent to hate him any longer. When one has brains and uses them, he begins to see both sides of every important question. I cannot help seeing the good side of Tipton as well as the side that is dangerous to me. I can't hate him . . . to save myself. Therefore, he is constantly on edge against me, because that burning hatred that he always feels never will allow him to close his eyes. It serves him as food and drink. He can eat that hatred as I would eat a good steak. It is a spur driving into him. And some one of these days, when I've lain down, tired out, that hatred will enable Tipton to drive up to me and get me. But, after all, the hatred of me is not the greatest thing that he owns."

"Then, what else is there?" asked the girl, fascinated by this strange harangue.

"Something that you would not think of, because you possess it, to a certain extent. The things we have never seem very important when other people possess them, you know. You're honest, and, therefore, the honesty of Tipton doesn't seem a very great matter to you."

"Honesty?" she cried. "Will you tell me how in the world honesty could ever help him to capture a. . . ."

"A crook? I'll tell you. The strongest man is the most natural man. A man who can walk better on his feet than on his hands, because the feet are meant for walking, you know. In the same way, we all have an instinct for doing the things that society demands of us. That is when we are at our strongest . . . when we're serving other people as well as ourselves. And that is why Tipton has a great strength in his honesty. For instance, I couldn't buy him off . . . I couldn't beg him off. If his sweetheart and his old father and mother were all to be saved from drowning if he would leave his duty . . . they would drown, but his duty would have to be done. He has only one eye in his mind, and that looks straight before him and sees the things that have to be done, in order that he may be able to look every man in the face. And that is a huge

158

matter with him. It means that he can look the world in the face, and it means that he can look *himself* in the face. A vast satisfaction. He loses no hours of sleep because of his past."

"And do you?" said the girl.

"Well, well," murmured Dunleven, "you will have me confessing my whole soul to you, before I'm done. But it's true. I've lost sleep because of my past. Yes, I've lost plenty of sleep, I can assure you. Now and then, no matter how well guarded one may be, one turns the corner and comes suddenly in sight of one's better self. And then there's the very devil to pay. Suppose Tipton should come on me at such a time? He would find my muscles unstrung, my nerves jumpy, my eyes dim. I would be helpless against him. Furthermore, to fight down these weaknesses and this tendency to return to the normal, and to regret the normal, I have to expend an amount of effort that will, eventually, make me old before my time, while Tipton will still be fresh and young.

"And so, my dear Nell, you begin to see what reasons I have for dreading this blond, handsome, stupid-looking fellow . . . this same Tipton of whom you think so little?"

She was in a brown study. "Everything that you say confuses me more and more," she said at last.

"Of course. Because I am showing you the whole truth. Half-truths, or whole falsehoods, are simple and clear and easily understood. But the whole truth is like a forest of trees. Or it is like a jewel with so many facets that one can never see half of them at once. The colors seem to be changing."

"Will you tell me one thing more?"

"A hundred, if you wish."

"When you see the truth so clearly, why do you remain living this life, as you do?"

"I'll tell you," said the outlaw. "I have my regrets. I envy every man his quiet, peaceful life. When I see a pretty, sensible, sweet girl like you, I want to settle down and raise a family. A damned good job I should do of it, too. However, on the other hand, I am tormented by hard rides, cold nights, starvation periods, a thousand enemies, and above all . . . by the great Tipton . . . for he is really great, though I suppose that even my testimony could never convince the world of that. But to balance against all of these things, I have the perverse and exquisite pleasure of doing the unexpected. Of baffling the other men. Of matching my hands against ten thousand hands. Of playing a great game that has not yet come to the last trick. Of mastering all these very difficulties which I have enumerated. All the prices that I pay are cheap for the great jewel that I am able to buy . . . freedom, freedom, freedom! My will is my own master. I do as I wish."

"Ah, yes," said the girl. "I understand." She nodded her head, with her eyes closed and pain in her face.

"You want to be free," sympathized the bandit. "You hate this drudgery. You are tired of slaving for that crotchety, sour-tempered, exacting father of yours, who takes everything for granted. You know that you have the looks and the talent to rule men and make a place for yourself. You feel that those talents are wasted here. Eh? Well, well! But you never could leave. Your honest soul would torment you to the end of time. You could never stifle the voice of conscience as I have done. You never could do it, Nell. Never! You haven't the strength."

She leaped to her feet, angry and excited. "Do you think that I haven't?" she said through her set teeth. "Ah, well, you don't know me any more than I knew you, when I first saw you. . . ."

"Go on," said the outlaw softly.

"No," said Nell. "No, I can't tell you."

"Too black?"

"Yes," she said. "It's too black a thing to confess even to an outlaw. But . . . I almost think that I'll do it." She roused herself. "Now you have to get away," she said.

"I do."

"I'll take you out and show you the field where I put your horse. It's a little pasture back among the trees. Nobody ever comes there. I didn't dare to let Dad see her, when he came home last night."

She led the way out of the cabin and across the clearing and through the woods to a small enclosure among the trees where the bay mare waited for them. There she watched her companion cinch on the saddle. He mounted.

"I shall not forget you, or what you have said," she told him soberly. "I shall always remember."

"Good," nodded Dunleven. "But there's one more thing that I forgot to add. I looked out of a cranny between the logs of the loft when big Tipton was riding away this morning. . . ."

"You weren't asleep, then?"

"Certainly not! As he rode over the hill he turned and looked back. . . ."

"But what of that?"

"Ah, you don't know Tipton. He never looks back, except when there's some shooting to be done toward the rear. He's not the type of fellow who turns his head a hair's breadth from the course of duty, as I said before, and duty this morning, as he thought, led him after me and across the hills. Now, my dear, if you need an interpreter, I'll explain the riddle for you. It simply means that young Tipton has found a girl whose face disturbs him. He's come across a dozen of them before. But none of them was the peculiar combination that was destined to knock at his heart and unlock the door to it. You, Nell, are the lucky girl."

"You are laughing, now," frowned Nell.

"Not a bit. There is your grand chance, Nell. Get him!"

"Is he richer than poor Dad?" she asked angrily.

"Money," said the outlaw. "It is money, then, that makes such a great difference to you? Is it money?" He shook his head. "Ah, Nell, there's the flaw in you, is it? I knew that something must be wrong, but I didn't know that the damage went so deep. Poor Nell. This . . . money. Of course!" He waved to the gloomy trees, then to her much patched dress. "I hardly blame you, Nell," he said. "But money? That's base!"

"It's what you rob and murder for!"

"Aye, but I'm a man, and not an angel. Good bye, Nell."

A little passion seemed to grip him. He put the good bay savagely over the fence and was instantly gone among the trees.

Chapter Ten

"PLANS"

At the edge of the wood, the outlaw paused. He had put this half mile behind him at such a round pace that one would have thought that he never again expected to see that part of the world. That was exactly the impression he hoped to leave in the mind of the girl, but, once he was fairly out of sight and hearing, he drew rein.

The wound of which he had talked lightly was in reality torturing him. To be sure, as he had told Nell Wooster, it was no more than a glance of the bullet along his side, but that was enough to torment him. The flesh was torn away from a narrow furrow, and the whole side was inflamed and swollen from his exertions of the night before. He could ride on a great distance, he knew, if he wished to force himself. But he did *not* care to force himself. He had endured enough pain in his life to wish to avoid new torments if he could, and he saw no reason why he should not be as safe in this wood as in any other place.

First, he rode in a brief circle that wound out upon itself until his trail was like an endless spring coiled upon the central point. One would have thought that he was cutting for sign, but, as a matter of fact, he was doing just the opposite. He was hunting for a place in which he could make his trail disappear.

He came, at the last, upon exactly the place he wanted. It was a narrow creek that cut down a slope at a good rate of

speed and had carved out a steep-sided gulley for itself. On
one side there was a broad ledge of rock—a gray stone that
was new to the eye of the outlaw. But it was as hard as
quartzite and took the shod fall of the hoofs of the bay as
though they had been mere pelting pellets of swan's down.
One would have needed a microscope to discern the traces
that the iron shoes left on that flinty surface.

Down this platform, the bandit continued for a quarter of
a mile. Half a dozen times he came to sharply shelving surfaces where it seemed impossible that a horse should have
gone. But in each place he dismounted and, with hand and
voice, encouraged the mare until he got her up or down to the
new footing. For she was agile in spite of her size and as docile
as a trained dog.

The course he took was upstream, straight toward the
head of the valley down which the creek poured. The farther
he continued, the ranker and thicker grew the underbrush,
and the taller and darker arose the trees. He could see why the
place had never been cut by the lumbermen. The bed of the
creek was too thoroughly blocked with jagged boulders for
logs to be floated down to the main river and thence to a saw-
mill. In addition, it would be impossible to drive a road
straight to the hills at this point. Far ahead he perceived the
white leap of the waterfall, dropping a hundred feet from the
edge of the cliff above and leaping in a dazzling cloud from
the rock that it struck beneath.

That precipitous rise blocked all travel through this
narrow blind alley among the hills. And since there was no
outlet here, it seemed fairly certain that no one would search
for him in such a direction. It was not likely that he would
travel into a pocket, if he could avoid it. And still less likely
was it that he would take hiding in such a place. Four men
well posted across the mouth of this valley could coop him

here until he starved. If he wished to go over the hills, he could only do it by leaving his horse and saddle and all behind him.

For these very reasons, he decided that the place was made to his order. Clever as Tipton had become on the trail, by dint of the long experience of the years, he was hardly apt to look for his quarry in such grounds as these. All that Dunleven wanted now was an adequate shelter.

He did not attempt to select some dark and dingy cranny among the rocks, where he would nearly die of depression if he did not die of the cold and the damp. No, for secrecy he relied entirely upon the nature of the valley itself. He selected as his temporary home a face of rock that angled sharply out from the cliff. He set against this some fallen branches that he found already prepared to his hand by the storms. Over these he threw fresh cuttings from the evergreens, woven together according to an art that he had learned in a rude fashion from an old Yaqui long years before. So arranged, the evergreens made a shelter that was stronger than it looked, and for a week or ten days it ought to avail him to turn the water and the wind.

This gave him a clumsy lean-to, long, dark, and narrow against the face of the stone. He brought into it a great pile of evergreen cuttings to make a bed and keep a fresh, dry stock on hand. Then he pressed through the brush and the trees until he found a place where the trees grew sparsely enough to admit grass, luxuriant grass, among them, and here he left the bay mare. He continued his work until he had found a rabbit at the edge of the woods. This he shot, and, bringing it back to his new home, he cooked and ate it to the last morsel.

When all this was accomplished, he heated some water and looked to his wound. In spite of the pain that it gave him, it was in better condition than he had hoped. He washed it clean, rearranged a bandage, and washed the old cloths in which it had been tied. After that, he settled down to an animal life.

He had no books to read. The valley was so cramped and small that he could have learned it by heart in an hour's ramble. Yet he was not bored or wearied by this life. But, like a wounded bear, he spent the time studying the progress that the wound made toward recovery, and watched the slow drift of time over his head. He slept much. He ventured out once each day, shot game, returned to cook and eat his single meal, and waited for the fall of another night, and then the rising of another day.

In this fashion, the time passed with him, and at length a week and then ten days had passed—and the wound was, to all intents and purposes, cured. He would not willingly have entered upon a hand-to-hand struggle with a strong man, at the end of this time. But although he was thin and a little weak from these days of quiet life, his spirit had grown calm and strong in this period of peace. The world had passed him in the distance, like a strong flow of water that keeps an echo about the house on the hill. It was never out of his mind, and yet it was never wholly in it. When he caught the bay mare again, he found her apparently like himself, younger, gayer, refreshed, and eager for her return into the world.

So he rode down the valley and came again to the more open country beyond. His plan was perfectly definite. He would drift to Denver. There he would make a change of clothes, and in an hour or so after his entry to the city he would be at a certain spot not far from the city limits, and where he knew that the grade slowed the eastbound trains to a creeping gait. That creeping gait might have seemed a dizzy enough speed to some, but, to Dunleven, it was just sufficient to enable him to enjoy the swing onto the iron ladder that would lead him to the top of a boxcar as the freight whirled past. Perhaps he would meet with an obnoxious shack, but there were ways and ways of *persuading* a shack to be kind, and he knew them all.

Perhaps he would need ten days, or perhaps he would need twenty, if he decided to take the longer but much slower routes through New Orleans and then north again. But at last he would be burrowed away in a safe quarter of Manhattan, where the shifting of the crowds provides a perfect screen for those who do not wish their movements to be seen.

After that, who could tell where the next move would take him? He might take ship for the farther side of the Atlantic where he had struck some excellent blows before this. Or he might drift to the West Indies, where there was much that needed doing from his point of view. Or, again, it was some time since he had followed the cold trails of northern Canada; Alaska was a land where his ugly face was fortunately not well known; and, always, he had the sunny land of Mexico to enter when on pleasure bent. Mexico, that he knew and loved so well.

Indeed, the trails of crime that his forebears had established hither and yon across the globe were now all open to Dunleven. He used them all, and he used them purposely. He had always had a feeling that, if he ventured to remain for long in the States, the inevitable Tipton would have a strong grasp upon him. But by whisking into the States and out again, he passed from the view of the ranger, and then swung back across his horizon again in a baffling manner.

The head of the outlaw was filled with these plans. The thought of Canadian furs, of French wines, of Mexican white walls, of island palms, and the roar of Manhattan traffic all mingled in his mind's eye. His wallet was filled richly with money. There were certain accounts, too, that were opened to him in various banks, under various names. These were friends that he could lean upon in times of need.

He started off gaily enough. Everything contented him. Above all he was pleased with the feeling that the ten days which he had spent in seclusion must have been enough totally to bewilder Tipton. Where the ranger might be hunting for him now, he could not guess. Or perhaps, as had happened a few times before, even the bulldog ranger had been forced to confess himself beaten and had gone back to report another failure to his captain.

Such things were well enough to sweeten the way for Dunleven, and yet he was not happy. He strove to understand some reason for this strange state of affairs, but reason there seemed none. There was a weight upon his mind, and, turning his head from this section of the country, he felt that he was leaving something of importance behind him, although what that might be he could not tell.

He came up to the crest of a wooded rise, where the trees thinned out, and, from this vantage point, he could scan a long ribbon of road that tossed up and down the length of a narrow valley at the side of a stream whose waters were yellow with a recent freshet.

A rider came onto this road around the farthest bend, swinging along at a racing gallop, and the outlaw, unlimbering his field glasses and bringing them to a focus, made out that it was a girl. Then, around the bend behind her, came a man riding in pursuit, it seemed, for every now and then the girl would look back and then urge her mount to fresh efforts.

He saw with the very first glance that the pursuer would win. There was too much quality in the long legs of his horse for the mustang that she bestrode to carry her out of reach.

Dunleven and the bay were in action instantly. He was not

a sentimentalist. Certainly he was no knight errant. But what he hated most in the world, perhaps, was to see the strong take advantage of the weak, whether the weak were women or men. The bay mare cut down the slope like a flash, and he halted in the last thick screen of trees just beside the road well before either the girl or her pursuer reached that spot. So, looking out through his covert, he received a sudden shock of rage, and shame, and satisfaction. For yonder rode a man who was a stranger to him, but the girl who flogged her failing mustang down the road was none other than Nell Wooster. Aye, and now, realizing that her game was lost, she pulled up her horse, almost opposite the place of the outlaw, and whirled to face the stranger.

Chapter Eleven

"A BARGAIN"

The savage satisfaction of Dunleven was increased. He had no desire to act suddenly. But he knew that this fellow was in the hollow of his hand. What a groaning and snarling and yelling there would be when the strong hand closed.

It began in a way far other than Dunleven had expected.

"Damn it," said the stranger, as he pulled up his horse beside the girl's. "Damn it, Nell, why did you run away?"

"Because I didn't want to talk to you," said Nell Wooster.

"A mighty poor reason, and you know it," said the other. "You might have known that old Fidget would run you down."

"I knew Fidget," said the girl, "and I knew that you would flog him within an inch of his life, if he didn't get up to me. But just the same, I hoped that I could get away, Chip."

"And why?" scowled Chip. "D'you think that I'm some moving picture villain? I haven't come to pester you, if you don't want to be pestered. I'm not in the position of having to do that. And you ought to know it."

She nodded.

"When I saw you yesterday," he said, "I told you to take a day and think over what I had said. You agreed that you'd talk today. But if you don't want to talk . . . why, hang it, you don't have to. Only, it made me mad to have you scamper off like that when you saw me. As though I was a dragon, or something. What's the matter with you?"

170

"Look here, Chip Dunstan," said the girl, "why do you really, down in your heart, want to marry me?"

"Why does any fellow want to marry?" he said.

"Part of 'em because they see that their friends are married," said the girl. "Part of 'em because they want a woman at home to fuss over them when they come in with wet feet and a cold in the head. Part of 'em because they want a home started. Part of 'em because they don't know any cheaper way of getting their meals cooked. And a few because they get silly about some girl."

"Always thinking things out, ain't you?" remarked Chip Dunstan. "Never seen a girl like you for thinking things out, Nell. Now, where do you put me on that list?"

"You don't exactly belong on that list," said Nell.

"Don't I? I'm glad that you see I ain't like all the dunderheads in this neck of the woods."

"I didn't say you were any better."

"Go on, then, and tell me what's what?"

"Why, since you bought the Crocker place on the hill, you think it's foolish not to have a woman there to run it and boss things around and dress fine and look like a rich man's wife."

"Bah!" said Chip. "That's a fine way for you to talk, Nell."

"That isn't the only reason," said Nell.

"No," he said, "because I've always intended that I'd marry you, someday. You know that."

"I know that, and I know why you wanted me, too," she responded.

"Tell me, then."

"Because you wanted something to show off and have over the rest of the men and their wives around here."

"Did I?" grinned Chip. "Ain't you a little fond of yourself, honey?"

"Oh, no. I don't say that I'm made of better stuff. I don't

say that I'm half as good as most of them, but I'm prettier than most . . . and I could be stylish enough to suit even a rich man . . . and you keep that in mind. Besides, I'm a little smarter. I could show you how to polish yourself up a little and get you ready to step around among some of the near-swells. You've had all of those things in your mind."

He stared at her, not embarrassed, but wondering. "That's it," he agreed. "That's what I've always felt and what I've always said. You think too much!"

"Right," she said. "And a good girl doesn't waste too much of her time thinking. I know that as well as you do. I've thought enough to get discontented with the shack and the way that we live in it. I've thought enough to make me pretty sure that I've got to have comfort. You know that. You would be ashamed to talk to an ordinary stupid, good girl the way that you've dared to talk to me before, and the way that you'll talk to me today. And that's why I wanted to ride away from you."

He nodded and smiled faintly again, running his eyes over her and the tired horse.

"Dog-goned if you're not a corker, Nell. You'd make a partner for a man, you would."

"Aye," Nell said, "that's just what I would. A partner, but not a wife, and I know it as well as you do."

"Ain't there *any* love in you, Nell?" he asked.

"Oh, yes," said the girl. "There is. But it would take a whale of a man to get it out of me. A regular whale of a man."

"There's no such man in the world," he assured her. "You can lay to that. You've fallen in love with some dream man. That's all. There ain't a chance of turning it into flesh and blood."

She laughed, and her laugh had an ugly ring in it.

"What if I were to tell you that I've *met* a man that I could almost love?"

He glared at her. "It's that tall blockhead of a ranger! It's that Tipton, who's always hanging around!"

"Is it?" she goaded. "Well, old-timer, you've guessed wrong."

"It's Tipton!" he insisted. "That big fat-headed. . . ."

"Stop it!" said the girl, flushed with anger. "He's a lot too fine for you to blackguard him. He's a lot too fine for me, too. I never met such a fine fellow in my life."

"There!" exclaimed the other. "You've admitted that he's the man. What's the matter? Can't you get him to the point of proposing to you?"

She fingered the handle of her quirt as though she were tempted to lash Chip Dunstan with it. Then she shrugged her shoulders.

"After all," she said, "it doesn't matter what you think. I've said that it wasn't Tipton. Now you can go ahead and flatter me with any sort of thoughts that you have on hand. I don't care!"

At this, he lifted his lean, homely face, and smiled again. "Well," Chip began, "let that go, will you? I don't care about the ranger. You're not going to him. You're going to me. I'll tell you why you're going, too. I'm going to bid so high that you won't be able to afford to refuse."

"Will you? You make me sad, Chip . . . you're so cock-sure."

"I've got reason to be cocksure. I know that a man has got to pay for class, when he wants to have it. That's why I outbid everybody else for the old Crocker place. Then, when the bargain was closed, what did I do? I added five thousand on top of what I'd agreed to, and wrote out the check in even figures. That's the kind of a man I am. I like to do things up hand-

173

some, Nell, when I put my mind to it."

She listened to this boasting thoughtfully. "That's partly brag," she finally said, "but it's partly true, also. You've always squeezed dollars till they screamed. But that was when you were out to make a fortune."

"Oh," said Chip, "and I'm still making it. You don't think that I'm contented with the sort of things that I've done up to this time, I hope? Because, I'm not. Not a bit of it! I'm a big man in this county, but that's not enough for me. I'm going to climb until I'm a big man in New York, too. I'm going to sit down on the inside circles and look through the windows at the crowd going past! That's me, Nell. You can throw away the dyed goat and wear sable when you hook a missus in front of my name! I'm going to kite you up like you were hitched to a balloon!"

"That sounds to me," admitted the girl. But it seemed to Dunleven that she turned a little pale, as though in disgust of her own speech. "Oh, I'm low enough to like that."

"I'll tell you what," said Chip. "I'm honest enough to admit that you're right. I need you. I pay for class. I paid for the Crocker place. I paid three thousand for this nag. Because I wanted the right thing under my saddle. You've got class, Nell, too. You ain't the greatest beauty in the world. You ain't got a great name. You started right down on my level, and you know what has to be done to my hands before they can be crowded into kid gloves. I could talk to you, man to man, and you wouldn't whine. Now I'll tell you what. When you marry me, you get your own bank account. A sweet one, too. You get your own rooms in the house. You get money to buy your own library, that you always been so keen on. You get your own horses. And . . . *you get your own time!* Understand?"

She looked him straight in the eye.

"How much?" she asked. "How much time shut of you and your business and your house, Chip?"

"Why, three months," he stated.

"Six!" she snapped. "Six months, or I won't listen."

"No! That would make a scandal. They would say that I'd married a woman that I couldn't keep in hand. . . ."

"Chip. Let me have the six months, and the remaining half of the year I'll be so fine to you that they'll all have to point me out as a model wife. I give you my word for that."

He drew a long breath. "I believe that you would," he said. "Now you prove that you mean what you say. You send that Tipton marching, and tell him that you never want to see his face again. Just them words."

"Not for ten million dollars," she said.

"By God," said Chip Dunstan, "then the deal is off right now. No, I don't mean to talk in that tone. I can't bully you, and I know it. But . . . I'm afraid of that ranger, Nell, and that's a fact."

"All right, then," said Nell. "I'll send him packing . . . but in my own words. And now . . . I want to ride home alone. So long, Chip."

Chapter Twelve

"THREE DAYS"

Down the road toward the house of old Wooster, the outlaw rode at a brisk gait, but, when he came fairly near to it, he turned aside into the trees and pushed the mare cautiously through the tangles of trees and underbrush. When he came in sight of the house of Wooster, he was not surprised to find the tall, strong horse of Tipton tethered near the door. From the tone of the girl, he had gathered that the ranger was probably at hand. And Dunleven could guess at the reason for it. When the ranger had missed the trail of his quarry, he had waited near the point where it had disappeared—and, while he patiently combed the country in the hope of discovering some trace of the bandit, here was the girl at hand. There could be no doubt that the two motives kept the ranger in this place.

Now, through the shelter of the trees, Dunleven saw Tipton himself come forth. The girl accompanied him to the door of the cabin, and there she paused and leaned against the jamb, with one arm stretched above her head. Their voices came faintly to the listening ear of Dunleven.

"But you haven't told me why you have to go, John," she said.

The big man merely smiled at her. "In my company of rangers," he explained, "we don't ask questions. But when we get the order, we just march."

"But somehow," said Nell Wooster, "it makes me terribly unhappy. I feel that I've done a wrong to you, John."

"No wrong at all," said Tipton. "I've told you that I love you, Nell. I've told you that nearly every day since the first day. And if that don't do you any harm, it don't harm me, either. An so we're all quits. So long, Nell."

"Wait a minute, John," said the girl.

"Aye," said Tipton, turning back.

"I want to say something," she said, "but I can't find the words that are right."

"I'm glad to stand and say nothing, and look at you, Nell."

"Is it the last time that I'll see you, then?" asked Nell Wooster sadly.

"Oh, no," said Tipton. "I'll be back, someday, and find out the name of your husband and the names of your kids. I don't give up friends so quick as all that, Nell."

"Good bye, dear John."

"Good bye, Nell," said the ranger, and, as he mounted his horse, she closed the door in haste, as though afraid to keep him in view too long.

He turned his horse straight into the trees, and Dunleven swung sharply in behind him.

"Tipton!" he barked.

The ranger stopped his mount with a jerk and stiffened in the saddle. "Aye, Dunleven," he said. "It seems that you've got me, after all. Is it what you've been waiting for, to take me from behind?"

"You know me better than you pretend," said the outlaw. "But just pass your word to me that you'll make no try for a gun, and then turn around, and we'll have a chat."

"You have my word," said Tipton. And he turned his horse about. Even though he knew that Dunleven was there, yet, when his eye fell on the outlaw, his nostrils quivered and his eyes flashed.

177

"Gad!" said Dunleven. "You're hot to get at me, old-timer, aren't you?"

"Never mind that," said Tipton. "This is another one of your days, but my time may be coming. I'm ready to wait again."

"Aye," said Dunleven, putting up his Colt. "You'll wait, and maybe you'll have me behind the bars, one of these days. Why the devil don't I finish you off, now that I have the chance?"

"Because," said the ranger, "rotten bad as you are, there's one thing that you're above . . . and that's murder."

"Ah? But you'd never admit that in a courtroom."

"Maybe not. In a courtroom you don't need any help from me. Now, what do you want out of me by talk?"

"A couple of questions answered, Tipton. The first one is . . . what makes you hate me so bad?"

"What makes any decent man hate you?" asked Tipton savagely.

"Well, that's a riddle to me. Go on and answer it?"

"Because the thing that makes life good for any decent man is living inside the law. And you're outside of it."

"Come, come," murmured Dunleven, smiling. "Law is just a name. Nobody could have all the love for the law that you pretend to have. Come out in the open and tell the truth. You've never given over a grudge for the times that I've beaten you. That's the answer. That's what keeps you traipsing after me all of these years."

"You're like the rest of the crooks," Tipton said. "You can't figure that anybody has motives better than yours. You think that everybody would be a crook, if they had the nerve to go through with it. Isn't that what you feel?"

"*Humph!*" said Dunleven. "Maybe I do. Maybe I do, without putting it into words as crisp as all that. So you're going to keep trailing me to the end of time for the sake of the law? Why, Tipton, when I'm caught, one of your superiors will find a way to jump into the newspapers and take all the credit away from you."

Tipton waved a big hand that dismissed such an idea to the uttermost limits of limbo. "What's newspaper talk to me?" he said. "If I take you, I'll know that I've done something worthwhile, you can bet on it. I don't want to know what other folks think about me. I want to know what I think about myself. That's what counts."

The outlaw urged his horse a little nearer and stared curiously into the face of his old antagonist.

"Aye," he said. "There's something in that. It's what puts you beyond me, Tipton, I'm free to confess. It's what makes me respect you, more than any other man that I've ever met. Well, old-timer, I hope that when the end comes, it will be with you and me fighting it out hand to hand. If I have to go down, I'd rather have it by you than by anybody else."

"You've had your talk," said Tipton, still watching the outlaw with narrowed eyes of suspicion and of disgust. "Are you through with me now?"

"Not quite. I want to talk about your own business, first."

"I'm tired of this, Dunleven. I hate the sight of your face and the sound of your voice. Hurry through it, will you?"

"I've come to see the girl, now. I've come to Nell Wooster."

The ranger gasped. Then his anger mounted to his eyes.

"There's nothing that a gent like you can say to me about a woman like her, Dunleven," he declared. "I want none of your talk about her."

Dunleven's even temper flared. "You damned blockhead!" he shouted. "I've got more than half a mind to let you throw away your happiness into the junk heap. I would, if it weren't for the girl's sake!"

Tipton faltered and blinked. "It's wrong for me to let you talk about her," he said at last. "I oughtn't to do it, I suppose."

"Tipton," said the outlaw, "did she tell you why you had to march?"

"She said that there was another man."

"Do you know what man?"

"What business had I to ask?"

"Tell me this . . . do you know the other men who come to see her?"

"Yes, some of them."

"Are they a good lot?"

"Yes. I like them all . . . except one. There's only one bad one in the lot."

"Tipton, the bad one is the fellow that's to get her, according to the present lie of the cards."

"Chip Dunstan?" grunted the ranger. "I won't believe that!"

"I tell you, it's the truth. Tell me what you know about Dunstan, and then I'll tell you where she stands."

"What right have I to talk behind her back and his?"

"You fool! Put your scruples in your pocket for five minutes, and listen to a little good sense, will you? I say Dunstan is booked to have her. Now tell me what Dunstan is."

"Have you seen him?" muttered the ranger.

"Yes. I've seen him and his tricky little rat eyes. Is he as bad as he looks?"

"He's worse, by a good deal. I'll tell you how he started. He was a faro dealer in Juárez, and he beat his boss out of about ten thousand. He jumped to Havana and had a lucky season on the racetrack, playing the ponies."

"I don't believe it!" said the outlaw. "A cur like that never had the courage to risk good money on a race that wasn't fixed."

"That's just what I mean," answered Tipton. "He spent half his money fixing the races . . . and the other half he bet. He had a hundred thousand when he got word that Cuba was a pretty feverish climate for him to hang out in. Then he blew and hit Manhattan. He tried the races again . . . working some of the pools. He had two hundred thousand when he come back West to his home country. And he had the sense to risk fifty thousand in the Caulkins Lumber Company. They'd put half a million to open up their track, but they needed a little bit more to complete the work. He put in the extra bit, and he held them up for a pretty near half interest. Well, that deal turned out *big*. Caulkins has brains. And the company is worth more than a million in hard cash, right today."

"I had no idea that he was as big a bird as this," Dunleven said.

"He's growing all the time," said Tipton. "He plays every chance that's really crooked and is legally safe. Why, Dunleven, when I think of him, you look almost like a good honest man to me."

"Thanks," said the outlaw dryly. "But now I ask you, Tipton, if a decent man like you will stand by and see a good girl tumble into the hands of a rat like this?"

"What can I do?" said the ranger.

"Nothing?" asked Dunleven savagely.

"Tell me where you collected all this interest in the girl?" asked Tipton.

"Why, you fool," said Dunleven, "she put me up in her house in spite of her father and in spite of you on the first night that you saw her. That's the sort of person that she is!"

"The blood on the floor . . . !" gasped Tipton.

"Was out of my body, you blockhead! She cut her finger

181

right in front of your eyes, and made you believe that was the cause of the blood. I lay in that attic and laughed till my sides ached to think that such a fool as Tipton was trying to catch such a man as me."

Tipton seemed all at sea. "By gad," he said, "I never dreamed that it was in her."

"You hate her for helping a crook, I suppose?"

"I love her for it more than ever!" broke out Tipton. "It's wrong, of course, but I can't help loving her for it."

"Then prove that, man," said Dunleven. "If you won't try to help her from the hands of this cur of a Dunstan, will you promise me to keep off my trail for a week while *I* try to help her out of the hole?"

"Keep off your trail . . . give up following you?" groaned Tipton. "I've sworn an oath to my state. I can't go back on that oath, Dunleven."

The outlaw reined back his horse with a snarl. "I'm tired of trying to save you from yourself!" he spit. "Now talk turkey. Will you give me your promise and see the girl saved, or will you keep on like a selfish fool trying to catch me, and let her go to hell . . . or worse? Why, Tipton, I overheard them! He wants to buy her for a show . . . like a horse . . . or a piece of furniture . . . and she's almost willing to go for the sake of getting rid of the mean life in that shack of a house, yonder. You understand me?"

Tipton wrung his hands. "I wish to God that I knew what to do. I wish that I could be told," he groaned.

"I'll tell you what to do. Give me that promise. I only ask for three days. Then you'll have your chance at me again. But before you take your chance at me, I advise you to go to the girl and tell her that you love her."

"I've told her that," said Tipton simply.

"Told her that!" snorted Dunleven. "Have you laid hands

on her and told her that you'd die if you didn't have her?"

Tipton gaped at him. "A lie like that!" he breathed.

"Aye," said Dunleven, "marriage is one long lie, and you've got to take the first step in lying before you can get into the blessed state. No girl wants to marry a man. She wants to marry a damned archangel. Have you tried to make her think that you're an archangel, you booby? No, but you're going to! Do you think that she would have coddled you with her eyes and her voice when she was saying good bye to you if she hadn't wanted to have you, really? No, she wouldn't. Now give me that promise . . . you'll keep off my trail for three days."

Tipton dragged off his hat, breathing deeply. He was like one whose sight has been seared by a flash of lightning striking at his very feet. "I suppose that I promise," he said.

Chapter Thirteen

"WHEELER'S OATH"

With that promise in his mind, like a purse of gold in a messenger's bosom, Dunleven started joyously away for his work. He had waited only to learn a few more details concerning the husband-to-be of Nell Wooster. And, when big Tipton had told him these things, and, among the rest, where the house of the rich man was to be found, Dunleven headed straight for it.

There in the shadows of the woods, that afternoon, he made the circuit of the grounds and made sure how great was this single property that had passed from the hands of the Crockers who developed it to those of Dunstan, who would exploit it. There was everything here that a man could want—acres and acres of woodland, of pasture, of rangeland, of farming bottoms. There was the great house built to stand there forever. And there were the barns and the sheds and all the outbuildings that clustered like an ample village as a background to the mansion.

When the gloom of the evening began and the lights shone, Dunleven, gritting his teeth in the outer gloom, asked himself why a secret scoundrel like this Dunstan should have such a treasure in his hands? What justice would permit such a girl as Nell Wooster to be added to the long list of his possessions? He asked himself this, and then he sat down to wait.

Yet the patience that had endured ten days of half-starved existence in the wilderness could hardly endure the single evening that he had to pass through before he sat unannounced in the bedroom of Dunstan.

The evening of that late September had turned cold, with a raw wind sitting in the northeast and sending the big, newly dead leaves of autumn whirling out of the blackness like futile little ghosts that pressed their hands against the brightness of the windowpanes, and then vanished.

Dunleven took note of these things, and now he stretched his hands to the fire. He had noted the kindling of that fire, laid in pathetic haste by some old retainer, inherited with the house from the Crocker family, there was no doubt. Now, the underlayers of resinous pine spurted blue jets of flame and filled the room with a cheerful chattering and delicious fragrance. The layers of oak above began to smoke and blacken and burn slowly at the edges, like the doughty stuff that it was, slow to begin, and long in the ending, of course. All this work of the fire was against a burly backlog, fresh-hewn, solid, nicely fitted to the dimensions of the hearth. A good bit of wood, as substantial, one might say, as the rising fortunes of the young master of the house. And yet—suppose that that backlog were broken up and tossed over the flames, how long would it last? Hardly as many minutes as it would otherwise endure weeks.

Such were the thoughts of Dunleven while he sat there, smoking at his ease, tapping the ashes on the hearth. When he heard a long, steady, assured stride coming down the hall, he decided that it was time to move. He tossed the cigarette into the fire. He stood up and glided to a tall, heavy red curtain that dropped from the very ceiling and covered the entrance to a little adjoining library.

Behind the division of this curtain he stood at wait, his revolver in his hand. He saw Dunstan enter, pause at the door with his head raised, scenting the tobacco fumes that had not yet vanished, and then stride to the fire, in front of which he stood with blackening face.

Dunleven, amused, could see the passion rising in his scowl and his jutting jaw. The master of the house had decided that someone among his servants had dared to smoke in the chamber of their overlord. He was preparing the scathing speeches that he would deliver. First he must discover the culprit, however, and here Dunstan started with hasty strides toward the door.

"Wait half a minute, Dunstan!" said the outlaw.

Chip Dunstan half turned, saw the glint of light from the gun that peered forth between the two folds of the curtain, and then reeled as though he had been struck, throwing his hands above his head.

"It's Parker!" gasped Dunstan. "My God, Parker . . . it's you! If you've come about your father, I swear, old man, that I did nothing but business with him. He begged for that loan. He begged for it, I tell you! I can show you a letter from him! I told him money was tight. I told him that I would have to make extra hard terms, if he insisted . . . Parker, how was I to know that the old man would get excited when the time to pay came? I didn't mean the talk about disgrace and exposure that I sent him. That's just a form letter to get money out of slow payers. But how was I to guess that your father would get . . . er . . . nervous . . . and kill himself for nothing? How was I to guess?"

"You knew that my father would pay," hazarded Dunleven. "He's always paid every debt that he ever contracted. You knew that he would pay, even if bad luck held him back for a little. Then . . . why did you start hounding him the minute that the money was due? You killed him, Dunstan. You killed him without mercy!"

"No, Parker . . . and for God's sake turn that gun another

way . . . or step out here into the light where I can see your face. You don't intend to murder me, Parker? Great God, an idea like that would never come into your mind . . . not to me . . . a friend like me that can set you up and make you. . . ."

It was not exactly the most craven kind of fear, it seemed to Dunleven. It was rather the excitement of a man who desperately has to lose a matter upon which he places much value. So it was with Chip Dunstan. Having the thought of death in front of him, it was not fear of the ghostly end of all things that moved him; it was the terrible regret for the work that he would leave undone, and the opportunities for fortune and place making which would be thrown away.

Dunleven stepped out into the light, smiling, and a wave of relief crossed the face of the master of the house.

"By God!" said Dunstan. "I really thought it was Parker."

"Keep up your hands, Dunstan."

"I've got to have a drink. Pour it for me out of that bottle with your own hands, if you want to. I've got to have a drink. This relief is too much."

"It may not be a relief," said Dunleven slowly. "Do you know who I am?"

"I don't care, as long as you're not Parker. I don't care, stranger. You've come to rob me and my house. Well, I never keep hard cash in the house. It's the bank's business to do that little job for me. But you'll find some first-rate silver . . . something in the line of oil paintings downstairs, they tell me. If you've got a moving van along, you might be interested in some old furniture. Help yourself to every little thing that you see."

"Why," said the outlaw, "you're cool. You have nerve, my friend. There's material to you, as an old friend of mine used to say, enough to make a good man out of. Instead of that . . . there's you."

"Not good enough for you, stranger?" snapped the money-maker. "Well, what don't you like?"

"I'll tell you in the first place that you're a fine case for hanging. But you're too clever to get the rope around your neck. The kind of crimes *you* commit wind up with old men committing suicide."

"That old fool! He's not on my conscience."

"You haven't any conscience," Dunleven said. "My own is pretty near the vanishing point. But compared with you, I'm a spotless angel, newly dressed for heaven, as somebody said. But to get to the point, what I chiefly object to is your matrimonial attack. Buying women is an old dodge. But very few have the nerve to try to buy a girl like Nell Wooster."

Dunstan blinked, and then shrugged his shoulders. "You're somebody," he decided, "and you know something. But what do you want with me?"

"I came here to kill you, Dunstan. I knew that you were a dog. I thought that I'd kill you, and remove temptation from the way of the girl. Sweep the dirt out of her path, you see? However, I'm a mighty tender-hearted fellow. I really hate to kill if it can be avoided, and, after looking you over, I've decided that you might listen to reason. Dunstan, I'll take your word of honor sworn to me now, that you won't marry Nell Wooster . . . and that you'll break with her tomorrow before noon. You do that . . . or I come gunning for you. You hear me talk?"

"Very cross," said Dunstan slowly. "Yes, yes, a very cross man. Are *you* going to marry her?"

"That doesn't follow."

"I think I'll tell you to go to the devil," said Dunstan. "I don't believe that you're man enough to do a murder, stranger."

"Look at me again," said the outlaw. "I'm not such a

stranger to you as all of this, and you ought to know me a little better than you pretend to do."

Dunstan peered, but then he shook his head.

"I'll refresh your memory, then," the bandit said. "You've seen my face on posters, before this."

"Vaudeville? Trick-shooting, eh?" said Dunstan, without alarm.

"No," said Dunleven, "wanted for certain killings, jail breakings, robberies, and such trifles as that."

Dunstan leaned across the table. "Ah," he said, "Dunleven."

"Now you know me."

"It alters things a good deal, I have to admit," said the money-lender. "Your remarks which seemed so unreasonable a little time ago now seem worth considering. Because if you're Dunleven . . . you really *would* kill me out of hand."

"With a most exquisite satisfaction, you worthless rat!" Dunleven pronounced, smiling.

"Well, sir," said Dunstan, sitting down and leaning back at ease in his chair, "if my promise will suit you, I'll give you my promise that I won't marry Nell Wooster."

"Raise your hand," said Dunleven. "If there's anything secret in your heaven or your honor, I'm going to find out. Swear by those things first."

"By the whole galaxy of the saints, if you want me to," Dunstan promised, and raised an obedient hand.

Chapter Fourteen

"THE GUARD"

When Dunleven had accomplished the first stage of his work, he retired to the forest not altogether pleased with himself. He felt that he knew two things. The first was that Dunstan would never dream of performing the promise that he had just made to break off his engagement to Nell Wooster before noon of the next day; otherwise, he would never have made the promise so glibly. The second thing that he knew was that of all the men he had ever known in his long career of crime, he had never met one so utterly lacking in all the qualities that made a man worth esteem as this maker of dollars.

Yet, again, what made the task that lay before him more pleasant was that this would be no simple affair. For Dunleven knew this third thing was not of the least importance—that Dunstan was a man of able hand, and perfectly capable of taking care of himself in an emergency.

So Dunleven retired to the forest and pondered the facts of the case. He should have acted at once. That much was clear to him. He should have given the rancher an equal choice of weapons, and then finished the matter at once. But, when he faced the other, he was held back by the terrible certainty that his skill with weapons was immeasurably superior to that of the man with money. Therefore, he had fallen back upon the other expedient. He felt that he knew it would fail. But now he had a wait until the noon of the next day before him. Those hours of waiting were not dull, however.

The Outlaw Redeemer

When he reached the trees, he did not go far. Distance was not what he wanted for safety. He climbed straight up a tall tree, and there he built for himself a sort of a crow's nest. It was not overly secure when the wind rose, as it did presently, and swayed the top of the tree back and forth with much violence. But from this position he could look through the thinned leaves of the trees before him and peer into the windows of the house of Crocker, that had so lately become the house of Dunstan, without as yet shaking off all of its original dignity.

And, at least, he felt that he was fairly safe from discovery here.

For who among the searchers, if searchers were sent, would dream of looking in a hiding place so childish as the top of a tree, in order to discover the famous evader of the law—Hubert Dunleven?

What they all overlooked was that there was a great deal of childishness in the mind of this same Dunleven. So the man of crime sat secure and watched events happening with great speed. First, there was a rush of half a dozen mounted men from the house. If that was not a charge of the spare servants and laborers around the house to spread the warning, Dunleven felt that he had turned fool and was unable to read the simplest letters of events as they were presented before him.

Presently more horsemen approached the house. They came in groups of twos and threes. If these were not the answers to the summons that Mr. Dunstan had sent out, Dunleven felt that he was more a fool than ever.

The way toward the house passed directly under the tree where he had taken refuge, and he found much amusement listening to the murmur of the voices that rose up to him. Then he heard one voice louder than the others, a deep and familiar sound: John Tipton!

He understood at once. The rumor of the threat that he had made against Dunstan had already circulated far and wide until at last it came to the ear of Tipton himself. The word of the ranger had been plighted to keep from the trail of Dunleven for three whole days, and that word, as Dunleven very well knew, was inviolable. However, there was nothing in the promise of Tipton to keep him from occupying the position of a guard, and now he was determined to take his post to protect Dunstan, in the profound hope that, while he occupied that spot, the outlaw might come within gunshot of him.

Dunleven, understanding, shook his head. It trebled the already great difficulties of his task. The rest might be known men, many of them, but Tipton was Tipton—always a handful. Now he was added to the already heavy burden that Dunleven had to bear. No wonder, then, that he listened more keenly than ever as the voices of the two men rose slowly toward the trees.

"He thinks that Dunleven won't take a try at him until noon tomorrow. He's going to stay put in his room all of that time. And that's why he's sent for you. He wants you to sit in that room with him until the time comes. You understand? You're to have anything that you want, if you'll do it. And put your price high, I advise you. He can afford to pay."

How perfectly in character was the voice of Tipton as it made answer: "It's only my duty I'll be doing, if I take charge of this game. There's no price to put on it. The state pays my wages, friend."

The state paid his wages—small ones, too. But nothing on the side must come to Tipton. The man from Devon would have felt more than half corrupted if he had taken such money.

In the meantime, a strange performance was beginning

around the house of Dunstan. Half a dozen horsemen had started to walk their mounts around the big house, moving at regular intervals. Here was Tipton, come out to superintend their order. By the starlight, the outlaw could distinguish perfectly the outlines of that big frame, and the seat a little aslant in the saddle.

Dunleven felt that he had seen enough. He knew that the maker of money had decided to break his word. He knew what measures Dunstan had taken to make sure of safety. He started to descend from the tree, when he saw Tipton ride down the bridle path followed by four other men. Inner guards were not enough, it seemed. There was to be an outer picket, also. At least, it was in this fashion that Dunleven interpreted what he saw and heard. He climbed down to the lower branches of the tree and waited there.

The rain had begun to fall—rain cold enough for November with rattling leaves winging through the trees, now and again. Dunleven was chilled and wet, but still he did not stir while he strove to untangle the confusion of his thoughts. But he was beginning to feel that defeat was certain.

He knew that, without a miracle, he could not break through that guard that was thrown around the house of the rich man. And he knew, also, that he had no other way of getting at the money-lender unless he took wings and flew over the line of riders, or, like a mole, burrowed under the ground. Since he could do neither of these things, he was about ready to admit defeat, climb down from the tree, regain his bay mare, and ride on his way, but at this moment he heard the beating hoofs of a single strong-moving horse as it came up the path.

Dunleven listened, and then he looked through the deep dullness of the rain and the night and saw the big form of Tipton returning from his work with the outer guard.

He acted on impulse. Nothing else could have made him attempt such a hazardous action except sheerest impulse working upon a spirit highly irritated. When the rider passed beneath the tree, Dunleven cast himself down.

He had not more than one chance in ten of striking the rider, from that distance. If he missed, he would hit the ground and get some broken bones, if not a broken neck. Kind fortune favored him. It was the ranger that he struck, and the heavy impact crushed big Tipton to the ground from the saddle. They landed with a shock that numbed the brain of the outlaw—it left the ranger senseless and helpless upon the ground. There crouched Dunleven in the rain, wondering why he had done this thing and what good could come from it? He stared up after the fashion of bewildered men, and a fresh shower of big drops, shaken from the tree, struck his face. That dash of cold water brought home to him the first inkling of the thought for which he had been waiting.

First of all, he tied the hands of Tipton, and, as the ranger began to stir and groan, the outlaw gagged him securely, heaved him into the saddle on the horse, and, mounting behind, rode again down the avenue.

He hoped to pass the outer line of pickets unseen, but, as he came near the gate, the dim silhouette of a rider drew out of the rain.

There was a shout—but no bullet. Apparently the dimness of the night had been great enough to conceal the fact that there were two riders on the back of the ranger's horse. For the rest, what was to be suspected of a rider coming *from* the house of Dunstan?

So Dunleven and his prisoner plunged heavily down the road till it joined the main county road beyond the next bend, where the mailboxes glimmered faintly through the night. After that, the outlaw turned into a thick copse, where he had left the big, patient bay mare. Now, riding his own horse, his hand on the rein which guided that of the ranger, he made for a little deserted shack that he had noticed among the hills earlier.

There he dismounted, and into the damp, dripping interior of the cabin he carried his helpless man. The horses were secure in the same big shelter. In a moment more, he had kindled a meager fire in a corner of the place.

It gave little more than a handful of flame. No heat, but light was what Dunleven wanted. While the ranger, with the gag removed carefully from his lips, sat wondering in a corner of the shack, his captor produced a pen and a little batch of thin paper and envelopes wrapped in oiled silk. He used a bit of rotten plank across his knees for a table, and he fell to working slowly, steadily.

Once he looked up and said: "Will you write something for me, old man? This cold has numbed my hand and. . . ."

The ranger smiled. "I'll write nothing for you!" he said scornfully. "That's too old a trick, Dunleven."

Dunleven, with a sigh, went back to his work, and every letter was drawn with the most infinite care.

"I see," said the ranger at last. "First draft of a forgery, eh? Is that it, old-timer?"

The outlaw shrugged his shoulders. "For a ranger," he commented, "you're pretty near intelligent. Just miss out by a mite, I guess."

He looked up again, a little later, and said with a fierce scowl: "Out of all of this mess . . . have you still got any hopes of Nell Wooster?"

"None in the wide world," admitted the man of the law.

"Well," said Dunleven, "if I should manage to put her in your way so that you marry her, don't let that stand in your way. I expect you back on my trail. I wouldn't know what to do without you to liven things up."

Once more he turned to his work, and this time it was making a copy of what he had first so carefully drawn out. Now, however, his hand did not move slowly. It spilled the letters easily from the end of the pen. He finished, looked at his work, compared it with the original, and then returned to his labor. Not once, but half a dozen times that work was repeated, and it was a full two hours later that he looked up with a groan of relief.

Chapter Fifteen

"WHAT MONEY CAN'T BUY"

When the mail was taken from the box of Dunstan, early the next morning, there was found an unstamped envelope addressed in a bold, strong scrawl. When Dunstan opened it, he read within:

> **Dear Dunstan,**
> This is scratched in haste. I am on the trail of great news for you, I think. That is why I have not come back to the house tonight and why I don't intend to come. It may be that I shall be at your house before eleven o'clock. If not, I want you to come alone to the little shack in the hills south of your place . . . the one with the red paint on it . . . or paint that looks like it might have been red once. Try to get there not before noon, or you'll spoil my plans. Come alone. And you'll need a good horse and some straight-shooting guns. Sorry to make this sound mysterious, but you'll understand when you arrive.
>
> *Adiós*,
> **John Tipton**

When Dunstan had read this over, he fell into a brown study. Then he called a servant and told him to ask among all the men who had been gathered as a guard to the house and discover if any of them had ever been familiar with the handwriting of Tipton.

A red-headed man was brought in presently. He said that he had been a cook for a company of the rangers where Tipton served, and he knew his writing well, and had had a chance to see a couple of reports that he sent in.

"Rum reports they was, too," he said, "and a standing joke in the company. Old Tipton would write in . . . 'Still trying for him.' And then sign his name. Or else he would write . . . 'Nearly got him. My wound will be well in a couple of weeks, and then I'll start again.' That would be his way of describing a fight where he'd nearly lost his life with a bunch of crooks."

"Look at this address. Is that Tipton's handwriting?"

"That's his," pronounced the other without hesitation. "I recollect it by the funny way that he had of making circles over his i's, instead of dotting them. Same with the periods. Sure, that's his. I'd swear to it. Have you got word from the old boy at last?"

For those who knew, Dunstan had been anxious because of his disappearance.

"I've got word from him," admitted Dunstan gloomily. "That's all I need you for."

Still he sat for a long time, pondering. This was not the sort of a letter that he would expect from Tipton. There was a note of braggadocio in it, almost. Certainly there was an air of gaiety. He felt that the real Tipton would never have taken such a veil of mystery about himself. However, there was the letter as a bald fact, and its handwriting sworn to.

At eleven o'clock, Chip Dunstan belted on his two best Colts, and took his truest rifle from the rack. But he had no intention of going alone. A man with money, he always felt, should know when to spend it with a wise profusion. A man with others to guard him was an idiot if he did not use them, so he picked out the three most celebrated shots in the little company that had responded to his danger call.

"Start out for the red shack, two miles back into the country yonder," Dunstan ordered. "When you get there, hide yourself in the edge of the trees overlooking the shack. And when you see me appear and go toward that house, have your guns at your shoulders and be all set for trouble. You hear me?"

They heard him, and they went. At the very edge of the woods they lay stretched while they saw Dunstan, just after the stroke of noon, when the shadows had drawn to nothingness beneath the straight stemmed saplings, ride out into the clearing near the shack in a big Mackinaw, with his rifle balanced across the pommel of his saddle, and his head covered with a tall Mexican sombrero. They saw him ride to the door of the shack and dismount, and stride in—and they saw no more, they heard no more, for a time. . . .

What Dunstan saw at the door of the shack was only a blankly empty interior. He spoke once, gently, and, again, aloud. Then, muttering an oath at such foolery, he stepped into the shack—and found the cold muzzle of a gun clamped against the side of his head. He looked askance and into the eyes of Dunleven.

"You've come to die," said Dunleven.

"Bah," said Dunstan, pale but calm. "I have enough money to buy off ten like you, even if I have broken my word to you. All right, Dunleven. I know you, and I'll pay big, if I have to."

"Will you?" smiled Dunleven. "I tell you, there is one language that money don't talk. There is one thing that money won't say. Ask him . . . he knows."

He pointed, and the charmed eyes of Dunstan saw Tipton

tied to a post, hand and foot and back, with a gag between his teeth.

"This," went on Dunleven calmly, "is knife work . . . because you have your own men waiting, out yonder, and I don't want them to hear a gunshot. But if you'll give me your blackguardly word again to fight like a man, knife to knife, I'll put aside this gun. And there's a witness, who'll be alive after your death, Dunstan, to tell whether you fought like a man or whined like the dog that you really are."

He pointed again to Tipton. There was nothing but rage and horror in the eyes of the ranger. And so he rested his hand on the butt of his own hunting knife.

Afterward, three impatient men saw a man in a Mackinaw and a tall Mexican sombrero step from the door of the shack, mount the horse of Dunstan, and ride away.

They thought he was a little shorter and wider of shoulder. But they were not there to make too many comments. Ten minutes later they closed on the cabin in disgust, and there they found Tipton with a white face, still bound and gagged. There lay Dunstan upon his back, dead. His hands were folded across the breast that the knife had pierced. His eyes were peacefully closed by the thoughtful hand of the outlaw.

That was the reason that Tipton resigned from the rangers. For he said to Nell Wooster on the day that she promised to marry him: "He did it mostly for your sake, partly for my sake, and partly for his own. And what he did was bigger than anything that I could ever do by catching him."

"Aye, a thousand, thousand times," said Nell Wooster.

"And do you know the reason it was so big?" said the ex-ranger.

"It was so brave, so generous, so. . . ."

"I think," aid Tipton, "that he loved you, too. Otherwise, no crook could have done such a decent thing."

He almost regretted having said that, when he saw her eyes grow wide and her look turn far off into the distance toward a new idea. But his own heart was too great and too open to harbor such thoughts for long. He sent in his horse and his guns to the Texas Rangers, and he swore that he would never ride in a manhunt again.

For heaven's sake, Tipton, wrote back his captain, **are you giving up a career you were born to? All your people have done this sort of work!**

He wrote back the one eloquent letter of his life: **They didn't know what I know . . . what money can buy, and what money can't say!**

And what do you mean by that? asked the despairing captain.

Tipton's answer was a mere postcard.

Come to my house and see!

But that was the end of the trail that, you may say, began five generations before.

MAX BRAND®

THE PERIL TREK

Max Brand has never been equaled for his tales of the Old West, tales that combine historical accuracy, grand adventure and humanity. This exciting trio of novellas includes the title story, Brand's final episode in the thrilling saga of Reata, one of his most popular characters. Reata has finally freed himself from master criminal Pop Dickerman, but then he meets Bob Clare, a man living under the constant threat of death. Clare enlists Reata's aid, but to help him Reata has to once again confront Dickerman, and this time there's no telling what might happen.

MAX BRAND

MEN BEYOND THE LAW

These three short novels showcase Max Brand doing what he does best: exploring the wild, often dangerous life beyond the constraints of cities, beyond the reach of civilization . . . beyond the law. Whether he's a desperate man fleeing the tragic results of a gunfight, an innocent young man who stumbles onto the loot from a bank robbery, or the gentle giant named Bull Hunter—one of Brand's most famous characters—each protagonist is out on his own, facing two unknown frontiers: the Wild West . .. and his own future.

___4873-6 $4.50 US/$5.50 CAN

Dorchester Publishing Co., Inc.
P.O. Box 6640
Wayne, PA 19087-8640

Please add $2.50 for shipping and handling for the first book and $.75 for each book thereafter. NY, NYC, and PA residents, please add appropriate sales tax. No cash, stamps, or C.O.D.s. All orders shipped within 6 weeks via postal service book rate. Canadian orders require $2.50 extra postage and must be paid in U.S. dollars through a U.S. banking facility.

Name_____
Address_____
City_____State_____Zip_____
I have enclosed $ _____ in payment for the checked book(s).
Payment <u>must</u> accompany all orders. ☐ Please send a free catalog.
CHECK OUT OUR WEBSITE! www.dorchesterpub.com

PETER DAWSON

LONE RIDER FROM TEXAS

The heart of the American West lives in Peter Dawson's stories, with characters who blaze a trail over a land of frontier dreams and across a country coming of age. Whether it tells of the attempt of an outlaw father to save the life of his son, who has become an officer of the law, or a shotgun guard who is forced to choose between a seemingly impossible love and involvement in a stagecoach robbery, each of these seven stories embodies the dramatic struggles that made the American frontier so unique and its people the stuff of legend.

- -

WINTER SHADOWS

Will Henry

From the very beginning of his long and illustrious career, Will Henry wrote from the Native Ameri-can viewpoint with authenticity and compassion. This vol-ume collects two of his finest short novels, each focused on the American Indian. The title novel finds a band of Mandan Indians facing the harshest winter in their history, while having to deal with an unscrupulous medicine man. *Lapwai Winter* is set in Northeastern Oregon at the time of Chief Joseph of the Nez Perce. A treaty is violated, the terri-torial rights of the tribe are revoked . . . and the threat of war hangs ominously in

----

THE LEGEND
OF THE
MOUNTAIN

Will Henry

Everything Will Henry wrote was infused with historical accuracy, filled with adventure, and peopled with human, believable characters. In this collection of novellas, Will Henry turns his storyteller's gaze toward the American Indian. "The Rescue of Chuana" follows the dangerous attempt by the Apache Kid to rescue his beloved from the Indian School in New Mexico Territory. "The Friendship of Red Fox" is the tale of a small band of Oglala Sioux who have escaped from the Pine Ridge Reservation to join up with Sitting Bull. And in "The Legend of Sotoju Mountain" an old woman and a young brave must find and defeat the giant black grizzly known to their people as Mato Sapa.